Mary Elizabeth Braddon

Like and unlike

A Novel. Vol. 3

Mary Elizabeth Braddon

Like and unlike
A Novel. Vol. 3

ISBN/EAN: 9783337046620

Printed in Europe, USA, Canada, Australia, Japan

Cover: Foto ©Andreas Hilbeck / pixelio.de

More available books at **www.hansebooks.com**

LIKE AND UNLIKE

A Novel

BY THE AUTHOR OF

"LADY AUDLEY'S SECRET," "VIXEN,"
"MOHAWKS," ETC. ETC.

IN THREE VOLUMES

VOL. III.

LONDON
SPENCER BLACKETT
(Successor to J. & R. Maxwell)
MILTON HOUSE, ST. BRIDE ST., LUDGATE CIRCUS
AND SHOE LANE, FLEET STREET, E.C.

CONTENTS TO VOL. III.

LIKE AND UNLIKE

CHAPTER I.

LIKE A ROMAN

LADY BELFIELD went back to the Abbey after having spent nearly a week in London, without having obtained any tidings of Valentine. He had not appeared at Wilkie Mansions; he had not written either to his mother or to his wife.

That anxious mother had looked through the newspapers every morning and evening, fearing to read of some accident to her son, but the papers had told her nothing. She had questioned Phœbe, who assured her that there was nothing unusual in Mr. Belfield's prolonged absence. He would tell them that he was going away for a week, and he would stop for a fortnight, without writing to his wife of the change in his plans. Sometimes he would send a telegram, but not always. It was his way.

His mother knew very few of his friends, and those few had left London. She had no means of obtaining information as to his whereabouts, yet she was intensely anxious to see him, to be the first to tell him of Helen's flight. She went back to her country home deeply despondent, dreading to re-enter the house upon which so dark a shadow had fallen. She had been away only a week, yet the sense of trouble and apprehension had hung so heavily upon her, that it seemed a long time since she had crossed that familiar threshold. She looked at the landscape with a vague wonder as the train drew near home, astonished to find the foliage unchanged, the light and colouring almost the same.

Adrian was at the station to receive her. If the landscape were unaltered, there was a marked change in her son. He looked thin and wasted, his eyes were sunken, and his cheeks colourless.

"I am heartily glad to get you back," he said.

" You see there was nothing amiss with Valentine. Your fears there were needless."

Nothing amiss! How keenly the falsehood of those words stung him as he spoke them ; but it would be the business of his life henceforward to deceive his mother, in the endeavour to save her from overwhelming misery. To betray Valentine's ghastly secret would be to break her heart.

" No, I suppose there is nothing wrong," answered Lady Belfield, " but I was disappointed at not being able to see him. I wanted to tell him that which he must be told sooner or later. It will be harder to hear it from a stranger. Is there any news of Helen ? "

This last question was asked in a subdued tone, like an inquiry about one who is dead.

" No ; nor likely to be, I should think."

" She has not sent for her luggage ? "

" No."

" That is strange."

" Don't you think, mother," Adrian began gravely, " that as this misfortune is without remedy—a trouble which no act of yours or mine can ever modify in the future ; for which thought and counsel can provide no help—it would be far best that we should never more talk of that trouble, nor of Helen.   She is gone from us.   Let us think of her tenderly and in silence, as of one whom death has taken from us, under saddest circumstances.''

" You are right, perhaps, so far as that silence will be best.   It makes one's heart ache to utter her name, the name she has disgraced, the sweet girlish name which seemed so suited to her girlish beauty," answered Lady Belfield, in slow and sad tones, as the carriage rolled along the road where she had driven with Helen only the other day, the same scent of autumn flowers, late-lingering wood-bine, travellers' joy, and wild thyme on the air; " but I am not going to think of her as among the dead.   I look forward to the day when her eyes will be opened to her sin, when I may take her back to my heart, crushed and broken, perhaps, but redeemed from among the lost.   I do not forget the parable of the piece of silver.   I hope to find my lost one before I die.''

Adrian did not answer. He sat looking at the tangled blackberry hedge, with its luxuriance of leaf and bramble, clusters of blossoms and fruit, in all its stages between bud and berry. The sky shone blue behind the tracery of branch and leaf. A newly turned field beyond sent up cool odours from the rich red earth. All things were beautiful in the stillness of afternoon, a golden afternoon, steeped in warmth and light; but in his breast there was not one gleam of hope.

Everything at the Abbey was ordered as of old. Lady Belfield's rooms were a haven of repose and comfort, full of flowers and perfume, and beautiful objects; all things in their right places, no confusion, no overcrowding of ornaments or furniture, not a discordant note amidst the whole. If externals could make the sum of happiness, Lady Belfield and her son had every reason to be happy.

She sat in the library with Adrian after dinner, and asked him to play to her. He chose the organ rather than the piano to-night, and played some favourite numbers from one of Mozart's masses.

Those solemn and pathetic strains had a soothing influence upon them both, and seemed to lift them above the region of their own troubles.

He was still playing when Lady Belfield started up at another sound from without, the sound of wheels in the avenue.

"It must be Valentine," she said, as Adrian left the organ and went towards the door.

"Don't be too sure of that, mother. It may be Colonel Deverill, or somebody from him."

They went to the hall together, and the bell rang just as Adrian opened the door. The carriage was a fly from the station, and the arrival was Valentine.

He kissed his mother, and shook hands with Adrian, as easily as if all things were going well with him.

"Here I am at last," he said, "and very tired."

"Where have you come from, Val?" asked his mother, looking at him anxiously in the lamp-light.

He was smiling at her, evidently ignorant of the

trouble that had fallen upon him; yet there was a change in him, his mother thought, a change which she could not define. Every feature seemed to have hardened and sharpened in outline. He had grown thinner, perhaps, and was worn with travelling and excitement of some kind.

"I have come from Paris. I went over there after the York summer. I was in a furious temper, and I felt that nothing less than a week's rest on the other side of the Channel would quiet my nerves."

"Things have gone wrong with you at York then?" said his mother.

"Damnably wrong. The horse I had backed proved a duffer. Where's my wife?"

His mother laid her hand upon his shoulder caressingly, and answered in a voice broken by tears:

"Come to my room with me, Valentine. I have something very sad to tell you."

"Put it into as few words as you can," he said. "Perhaps I can guess it. She has run away from me, I suppose."

"Yes, Valentine. She has left you. How came you to guess——"

"Oh, only because the kind of thing is fashionable—and she liked to be in the fashion. Don't look at me like that, mother, for God's sake. Whatever I may have to bear, I can bear it best by myself. Nobody can lighten my burden for me. Come now, I'll make a compact with you. Don't you ever speak to me about Helen, and I'll never plague you by any complaints. If you—and Adrian—like to have me here, I'll come and go as I used when I was a bachelor, and let the past three years be wiped off the slate. Forget that I have ever been anything but what I used to be before Colonel Deverill took Morcomb."

"Of course we shall like to have you here, Valentine. This is your natural home, and here you are always welcome."

"Thank you, mother. I shall sell the furniture, and get rid of my Kensington flat as soon as I can."

He had taken the matter so coolly, had dismissed the subject so briefly, that his mother wondered at the ease with which the bad news had been broken, and when she went back to the library with her two sons, she felt as if the burden of grief had been lightened. No doubt it was wisest to try to forget; to forbid the utterance of a fatal name. Let life slip back into former grooves, if possible. Valentine would have his old occupations, his old amusements, horses, dogs, guns, country race meetings, occasional holidays in London with college chums. His life need not be empty or purposeless, even after this great sorrow. She did not contemplate the legal consequences of a wife's infidelity; the possibilities of a release for the injured husband. Her tender nature took only the woman's view of the circumstances, and to her such a loss and such a sorrow were enough to darken a lifetime. Her younger son, therefore, had a new claim upon her love.

She gave him Helen's unfinished letter, when they parted that night, without a word, and he was equally silent about it next day.

He never re-entered the rooms he had occupied with his wife, but resumed possession of his old quarters over the billiard-room—the rooms that had been his from the time he left the nursery, a bed-room and dressing-room adjoining, with windows looking into the stable yard, windows from which he could watch his horses being washed of a morning or taken out for exercise, and from which he could give his orders to the grooms. These rooms were remote from the library wing, had another aspect, and belonged to a different period of architecture.

In a week, Valentine had settled down to his old life, and was going out cub-hunting every other morning. He was dull and silent of an evening, tired after his early morning with the hounds, and he seemed to have lost a good deal of the elasticity of youth; but, upon the whole, his mother felt very well content that things were no worse with him. It was an unspeakable comfort to her to have him under her roof, to see him resume the old life. She did not know of the sleepless nights—the awful hours when the house was wrapped in darkness, and the sinner paced his room, alone with the memory of his sin.

Between Valentine and his brother there had not been one word about that fatal night. Adrian had felt that silence—complete silence—was alone possible. To live together in peace they must both studiously avoid every reference to that hidden crime; they must both appear to forget, albeit both knew that forgetfulness on either side was hopeless.

CHAPTER II.

NEARLY six weeks had passed before there was any sign from Colonel Deverill. He had left Scotland before the telegram reached Glasgow. He had been yachting in the Mediterranean, and the message had been delivered to him finally, after many vicissitudes, at Ajaccio. After that he had lost no time in crossing to Nice, and making his way to England and Belfield Abbey.

There was not much that he had to say when he arrived, and very little that could be said to him. Valentine was gloomy and reticent.

"Talk cannot do either you or me any good," he said, when the Colonel grasped his hand, and threatened to become effusive. "I am very sorry for you, and I have no doubt you are sorry for me. That is about all that can be said."

"But—but—I should like to know all that

there is to be known about this infernal business. Poor deluded girl! Surely you must have seen her danger, you must have had some cause for suspicion."

" I had none, or I should have looked after her better. I trusted her implicitly, and thought she was safe with her elder sister."

" Leo is a noble creature," said the Colonel, " but she is frivolous. She has been spoilt, Mr. Belfield. All beautiful women are spoilt, nowadays. There is an open homage paid to beauty which must deteriorate character. I don't think you quite realized what a lovely woman you had married, and how inevitable it was she should have admirers."

" I thought my honour was safe in her keeping, Colonel Deverill. That was my only mistake."

" Have you heard of her since she left here ? "

" Not a word."

" I telegraphed Leo to meet me at Waterloo this morning, and we had half-an-hour's talk before my train started. She thinks St. Austell is the man."

"I don't suppose anybody has any doubt about that."

"You will apply for a divorce, I suppose?"

"I suppose so, eventually."

He answered with a gloomy indifference which raised him in his father-in-law's estimation. He was evidently in no eager haste to shake off that dishonoured tie, to free himself for second nuptials. He was not a pleasant young man, but in this matter he acted generously.

He showed Colonel Deveril Helen's unfinished letter, telling him how the housemaid had found it on the morning of her disappearance.

"Wretched girl, it was like her to leave an unfinished letter," said the Colonel, "and half an explanation. God help her with such a protector. If I had been more among beaten tracks on the Continent, I might have met them—or heard of them; but I was not often upon terra-firma after I left Marseilles."

Lady Belfield begged the Colonel to remain at the Abbey as long as he liked; and he accepted her hospitality for three days; during which time he tried to discover further particulars of his daughter's flight, but could hear very little, although he had several conversations with Mrs. Marrable, and more than one chat with the woman at the Lodge, whose husband was employed in the garden.

No one had heard her leave the house—of that Mrs. Marrable was certain.

No one at the Lodge had seen her go out of the gate ; but there was a gate in the fence about half a mile from the Lodge, a gate which was sometimes locked and sometimes not, and she might have gone out that way. No such thing as a carriage had been seen waiting about upon the road near the park gate, either late in the evening of the 19th or in the early morning of the 20th.

This fact did not surprise the Colonel, as he had been shown the telegram purporting to be sent by Mr. Belfield, and no doubt despatched by some agent of St. Austell's. If Helen had known that such a summons was to arrive in order to facilitate her flight, she had lost her head at the crisis, and had anticipated the intended hour of departure.

She must have walked all the way to the station in the early morning, before any one was about to notice her. Colonel Deverill was tempted to make further inquiries at the station, where a young and beautiful woman starting alone by an early train would most likely have attracted somebody's notice, even if she were not recognized as Mrs. Belfield of the Abbey; but he shrank from an investigation which would lay stress upon his daughter's infamy. What good would it be to him to learn the details of her flight? The evil was done; she was a disgraced and ruined woman; she had eloped with a notorious profligate, and a married man into the bargain, a man who would not be free to make her reparation were her own bonds broken to-morrow.

The Colonel shrugged his shoulders and gave up his daughter to perdition. He would have helped her if he could; he would have taken her back to his heart as tenderly as the Vicar of Wakefield received his deluded daughter, could he have found her in remorse and abandonment. He had been very fond of his children, after his own kind of fondness—as beautiful creatures flitting about his house and brightening it—but he could not move mountains. If his daughter had gone wrong, it was not within his power to bring her right again. He shed a few fatherly tears over her fall; but he was inclined to resent the perversity of Providence which had turned all things to evil in his younger child's destiny.

"She might have been mistress of this fine old place," he told himself, as he smoked his after-breakfast cigar in the cypress walk, "but she must needs throw herself at the head of the younger brother; and then she cannot keep her silly little head in the vortex of a London season, and elopes with the very worst man she could have chosen. She might have gone off with a Duke, by Jove, if she had liked—a Duke who could have made her a Duchess in good time—but she chooses St. Austell—St. Austell, whose property is mortgaged up to the hilt, and who has a wife he can't get rid of."

The case was hard, and the Colonel's spirits sank as he dwelt upon his daughter's fate. He was not a man to add to his affliction by taking to himself blame in the matter. He felt that Providence had dealt hardly with his daughter, that was all.

The Abbey was beautiful in itself and its surroundings, and life went as smoothly as upon velvet, administered by an admirable cook and irreproachable servants in every department, presided over by a woman who was still handsome and whom he had once adored, whom he might still adore had he been in his usual spirits. But the Colonel was weighed down by gloomy thoughts, and those picturesque gardens had a funereal air, and the cypress walk suggested a place of tombs. Even the babble of the river had lost its soothing power. The Colonel flung his half-smoked cigar into the stream with a groan, and stood idly watching the movements of a heron on the opposite bank, until it spread its wide grey wings, stretched its long neck, and skimmed away seaward. He was not interested in the bird, but watched its movements in a dull lassitude of mind and body.

He made up his mind to start for London next day, but before he went a morbid curiosity prompted him to ask Lady Belfield's permission to see his daughter's rooms—the rooms from which she had stolen away unseen by any one, like a thief in the night.

"I suppose they have not been much altered since she left," he said.

"No, there has been nothing changed. No one has occupied the south wing since that sad day. I'll show you her room myself, if you like," replied Lady Belfield, feeling for him deeply in his affliction.

Mrs. Marrable brought the key of the outer door, which had been kept locked, and Lady Belfield and the Colonel went into the room together. There had been no changes mode,  except the usual covering of furniture and pinning up of draperies which mark the care-ful housekeeper. On one side of the room stood two large basket trunks, covered with black leather, on which Helen's initials were painted in large white letters; a smaller box for bonnets, a travelling-desk, and a travelling-bag.

"Strange that she should not have taken some means to get these things sent after her," said the Colonel, contemplating the luggage.

"She has been afraid to ask for them, perhaps."

"Yes; that is it, no doubt. But it was rather a feeble proceeding to pack everything so carefully, and then to make no effort to get the things away. Poor Helen! It is so like her."

He took up the travelling-bag, which was large and heavy, made of crocodile leather, clamped with brass, and provided with all the latest improvements. He had reason to know the bag, for it was his own, and only, wedding gift to his daughter, and it was not yet paid for; he received dunning letters about it every three months, and he felt that there must eventually be a settlement somehow. And to think that she had left it behind her, not valuing it any more for all the trouble it had cost and was likely to cost him. He felt more injured at the thought of this ingratitude than if he had paid for the object with solid sovereigns.

He opened the bag, and looked dreamily at the silver-gilt stoppers, the ivory brushes and glove stretchers, and shining cutlery. All her little luxuries of the toilet had been packed in this receptacle. White rose and eau-de-cologne, lavande ambrée, attar of roses. A cloud of perfume came out of the bag as he opened it.

"There may be letters or papers of some kind that may help us to find out a little more about her plans," he said.

"Don't," pleaded Lady Belfield, stretching out her hand entreatingly, as if to stay the violation of a secret; "what good can it do to know any details? She is gone—we cannot hope to get her back yet awhile."

"My dear friend, it is my duty to know all I can," replied the Colonel sternly, and thereupon he proceeded to ransack the bag.

He turned out all the treasures, the bottles, and brushes, and thimble-cases, and brooches and bracelets in their morocco boxes, treasures of ivory, of crystal and gold, of agate and silver. These he flung ruthlessly upon the dressing-table, and then with cruel hand he searched the silken pockets, until he found what he wanted, a letter, the last that St. Austell had written to her.

It had been written after their long talk by the river. It recapitulated his instructions as to her flight, explained the trick of the telegram which was to summon her to London in her husband's name, told her how he should be waiting for her on the up-platform—South-Western—at Exeter, advised her to take her luggage with her, and then after being strictly practical, the man of business vanished, and the passionate lover repeated his assurances of an undying love, a devotion which should know no change—urged her for his sake to be bold and firm, to fear nothing, think of no danger, remembering that in a few hours she would be safe in his arms.

" For God's sake, do not falter," he wrote. " I think I have proved myself worthy of your trusting love, by a devotion which has stood firm against every discouragement. You have given me your promise, my darling, the sacred pledge of responsive love. It would be as dishonourable as it would be cruel to break that promise, and to break my heart at the same time. I cannot live without you."

"I may as well keep that letter," said Colonel Deverill, when he had read it and given it to Lady Belfield to read after him. "There would be no good in showing it to Valentine."

"No, there would be no good. Pray keep it from him. There is nothing I dread so much as a meeting between him and Lord St. Austell."

"Oh, the days of duelling are past. There is nothing to be feared nowadays, except the Divorce Court and the newspapers. Publicity is the fiery dragon that lies in wait for the sinner."

"With a man of my son's temperament, there is always reason for fear," said Lady Belfield gravely. "He has taken his trouble very quietly—too quietly, perhaps. I should fear the worst consequences if he were to meet Lord St. Austell."

The Colonel shrugged his shoulders.

"I fancy you measure your son's feelings by an old-fashioned standard," he said. "The young men of the present day take all things lightly. A man gets rid of one wife and marries another within two or three seasons. The change is made so easily that one-half of society knows nothing about it, and the other half takes no notice. If your son meant mischief he wouldn't be here hunting and shooting. He would be half-way to Ceylon in pursuit of his wife and her seducer. He would be hunting them, Lady Belfield, instead of Devonshire foxes."

Colonel Deverill left the Abbey in a very despondent state of mind.

"I am a broken man, my dear friend," he said. "I have been tottering for a good many years; low in health, in spirits, and in purse; but this last blow has annihilated me. Leonora is a splendid creature, but she is the essence of selfishness. She lives her own life, and cares about as much for her old father as she does for the gatekeeper in the Park. Helen was always fond of me. Her disgrace will bring my grey hairs with sorrow to the grave. I don't feel as if I could ever hold my head up again among my old chums. I have boasted of that girl—I have been so proud of her. I shall go and hide myself at Kilrush. The cottagers and squireens will point the finger of scorn at me—but that won't count."

"You might almost as well stay in Devonshire as bury yourself at Kilrush," said Lady Belfield, pitying him in his desolation, feeling that she would like to comfort him if it were possible.

"Oh, but I have ties in Kilrush—ties of some kind. I have a stake in the country. The soil is mine, and though it pays me no rent it belongs to me. There is something in the sense of possession. Otherwise, for choice, I should infinitely prefer Chadford. There is a furnished cottage near the river which would suit me admirably."

"You mean the white cottage with a thatched roof and a verandah all round?"

"Yes, that is the place. Has it been long to let?"

"Only since June. It belongs to two maiden sisters. One of them was ordered to Germany for a rheumatic affection, and she and her sister went off last Midsummer, leaving their cottage in the hands of our local agent, who never has been known to find a tenant for anybody. The house is to be let for a twelvemonth, and for very little money. You had better take it, Colonel Deverill."

"My dear Lady Belfield, there is nothing I should like so much as to be near you, but you must consider that this neighbourhood would be full of painful associations for me, and that my presence would be full of painful associations for your son Valentine. Therefore, my best course is to bid you good-bye, and take my poor old bones off to Ireland."

CHAPTER III.

CAPABLE OF STRANGE THINGS

Colonel Deverill's brief visit being ended, life at the Abbey resumed its old course, each of the brothers following his own particular bent; the elder secluded with his books, his organ and piano; the younger devoted to sport, and living for the most part out of doors. It seemed sometimes to Lady Belfield as if Valentine's married life had been an evil dream, which had vanished with the morning light: as if all things were again as they had been before the Deverills. came to Morcomb. Yet this was but a momentary feeling, for although all the details of her daily life with her two sons were almost exactly as they had been, there was a change in the spirit of her life, a change which involved all the difference between happiness and unhappiness. The brothers were not the same as they had been in their mutual relations. There was something wanting, as if some subtle mystic link had snapped and left them wide asunder. They never quarrelled. There was no sign of angry feeling between them; yet to Lady Belfield it seemed that brotherly love was dead. Adrian was especially forbearing to Valentine; never did anything to provoke him, or resented any rudeness of his brother's; but there were no signs of that affectionate sympathy which had once been so sweet to the mother's eyes. She never saw her sons linked arm in arm, strolling up and down the lawn in front of her windows. She never saw Valentine lolling in at the library window to talk to Adrian, trying to tempt him away from his books, as she had been used to see him almost daily in the time that was past. There was a change in the spirit of both brothers, as if both were haunted by the memory of an unspeakable misery. A woman had come into their lives and poisoned all things for them. A woman's fickle love had blighted them both.

Never since that first evening of his return had Valentine spoken of his wife. For the first few weeks he had put on a spurious gaiety, had tried to convince everybody that he was in excellent spirits, and unaffected by his loss. The men who met him out hunting—men who had known him from his boyhood—found these forced spirits painfully oppressive. Then there came a gradual change, the forced hilarity died away, and was followed by a settled gloom. He hunted three times a week, and shot over the Abbey preserves; but he went nowhere, and refused all invitations from old friends and acquaintances in the county. He refused an invitation to spend a week at Wilmington, where pheasants were more abundant than anywhere else within a hundred miles.

The Miss Toffstaffs were indignant at such folly.

"Why doesn't he divorce his runaway wife and have done with it?" exclaimed Dorothy. "It is absurd that he should make so much more fuss than other men. And his brother is just as bad. Mother has asked him to dine and sleep three times since last August, and he has made an excuse for refusing each time. They are a couple of savages."

"Sir Adrian has been nowhere since his sister-in-law's escapade," said her sister. "I suppose he never got over his attachment to her, though she jilted him so shamefully."

Everybody in the neighbourhood was outraged at Sir Adrian's secluded life. Since that awful night he had isolated himself so far as it was possible from his fellow-men. He would hold no converse with men whose consciences were clear. It seemed to him that his knowledge of crime—his guilty reticence—made him a creature apart. He would not mix in society under false pretences. He would not give his friends the power to say by-and-by, should this dark secret be brought to light, "He had no right to come among us—to touch our hands and sit beside our hearths—knowing what he knew."

Again, he would not make the distinction between his brother and himself more marked than it need be. Valentine held himself aloof from every one, and darkened no man's threshold. Valentine's brother accepted the same isolation; with a single exception, and that was in favour of Mr. Rockstone.

The Vicar was his chosen friend. He never shrank from crossing the Vicar's threshold, knowing that in that house, had he dared to unbosom himself, he would have found sympathy and promise of pardon. He had often longed to unburden himself of that dreadful secret, to confess all, knowing that his secret would be safe in priestly keeping; but although there would have been infinite comfort in such confidence, he felt that his duty towards Valentine constrained him to silence. It was not of himself, or of his own feelings that he had to think, but of the criminal who had put himself in peril of the law's last penalty.

Seeing her two sons bent on isolation, Lady Belfield withdrew from society as much as she could without giving offence to her neighbours.

She still kept up her old intimacy with Mrs. Freemantle, and worked with her among the poor of Chadford Parish, which was a large one. She received all callers with her accustomed cordiality, and afternoon tea in the Abbey drawing-room or in the Abbey grounds was as pleasant as of old.

But there were no more dinner parties, and Lady Belfield declined all invitations.

"I am getting an old woman," she told her friends in confidence. "This sad trouble of my son's has aged me by ten years, and I feel that the fireside is the best place for me now."

At which a chorus of matrons and maidens protested. "*Dear* Lady Belfield, how *can* you say such a thing?"

It was the season of snipe and waterfowl once again, a wintry season, a time of grey, rainy days, varied by light frosts, and Valentine Belfield was spending a good many hours of his life upon the river or on the marshes, with his gun and a couple of spaniels. The low level marshland and the grey autumnal mist suited his humour better than a fairer landscape or a summer sky. He pushed his boat along the stream, or waded across the marsh, in a dull vacuity of mind, thinking of nothing, caring for nothing, except just to keep moving about in the open air. All keen delight in sport had departed from him. He only pursued it because it was necessary to him to be up and doing. He was sorry that he was not a soldier, obliged to obey orders, to make forced marches under a tropical sky. Sometimes he even thought of running away and enlisting in a regiment that was under orders for active service. Sometimes he thought of going out to Australia and digging for gold, or to the Cape to dig for diamonds. There would be excitement in such a life as that, he thought; excitement which would help a man to forget.

He would have carried out one of these plans, perhaps, since he loathed the dull quiet of his present existence, but for one restraining influence. He dared not go far from the spot where his secret lay hidden. He dared not leave the neighbourhood of that silent pool under the rushes, where his murdered wife was lying. He had an idea that were he to leave the Abbey the body would be discovered the next day. During the brief interval after the murder, in which he had been absent from the Abbey, he had suffered an agony of apprehension. To leave the spot again would be madness.

He had passed the basket-maker's cottage a dozen times, sometimes drifting slowly by in his boat, sometimes passing it on foot by the causeway. The place looked just the same as of old, except that no woman's figure appeared at the door. There was no smoke from the chimney, no sign of life. Old John was trudging about with his baskets, no doubt.

Having passed so often and seen no change in the aspect of the place, Valentine got out of the way of looking at it as he rowed by, and forgot his old interest in the poor, tumble-down cottage; but one November afternoon, while he was rowing slowly by, one of the spaniels gave a short, sharp bark, and an instant after he heard the shutting of a door.

"There's some one there," he thought; "old John, most likely. I may hear something of that Jezebel."

He moved his boat to the causeway, sprang on shore, and went to the cottage. He opened the door, and found himself face to face with Jezebel herself.

Altered since she left Belfield Abbey : altered for the worse or the better? He could scarce decide which, as he looked at her with rapid scrutiny.

She looked considerably older than when he had seen her last, in her housemaid's livery, the coquettish mob-cap, red gown, and muslin apron. She wore a cap to-day, but a cap of a peculiar pattern, pinched and plain, made of lawn, Quakerish, Puritanical. She wore a black gown, with a long straight skirt.

"So you have come back, Mistress Madge," he said. "Are you living here?"

"No, Mr. Belfield. I am only here for two or three days to look after my old grandfather."

"You are a very nice person. I am indebted to you for some of the happiness—and most of the misery of my life," said Valentine, flinging himself upon the bench beside the door, the bench upon which he had sat years ago, when he was in love with this girl. "Your anonymous letter brought things to a crisis."

"I am not sorry I wrote it," said Madge, with

a proud carelessness. "I was tired of seeing your underhand conduct. I wanted Sir Adrian to know what his sweetheart and his brother were worth."

"You mean that you were consumed by jealousy, and you wanted to do all the harm you could," retorted Valentine.

"You may say that of me, if you like. I shall not try to convince you differently."

"Oh, you are moustrous proud and prim. You have turned hypocrite, and are full of pious cant, I have no doubt. You belong to some sisterhood, I suppose."

"More than that, I have founded a sisterhood."

"Indeed."

"Yes. I and a handful of women like myself—there are just twenty-two of us now—have established ourselves as nursing sisters among the fallen and the unhappy—among broken-hearted women. We seek out those cases of abject misery which seem to lie outside the limit of ordinary help."

"What do you call yourselves?"

"Sisters of the Forlorn Hope. We have a

house in a poor neighbourhood which is called the Forlorn Hope, and which we use as a refuge for unhappy creatures who have no other shelter. It is small, but we hope to make it larger."

"Of course, and you spend your lives in begging for funds, I suppose."

"We are not ashamed to beg; and we find that people are very kind to us. Half our funds have been gathered among working people who can ill afford the pence they give us, but the good has been done all the same."

"And your fallen women?" asked Valentine, with his cynical air. "Are they pleasant patients?"

"Not always; but they are rarely ungrateful."

"And when they are well—they go out into the world and forget all you have done for them, I suppose?"

"Not always. There are some who remember us, and who help us, with their small means and large hearts."

"And you really believe you have made conversions—that some of your fallen women have walked straight after your administrations?"

"Yes, we know of some who have tried to lead better lives; but most of those for whom we have cared were marked for death before we found them. We have been able to smooth their last hours. That is at least something."

"May I ask what it was that inspired you with the idea of this mission?" asked Valentine, looking at her wonderingly.

She was completely in earnest; she had that grandly resolute air which he remembered of old— an air that made him feel a shallow trifler in her presence.

"I was with my mother all through her last long illness and till her death," she said. "When she was gone, I made up my mind to devote myself to—such death-beds, for love of her."

"She had not been such a very good mother that you should devote your life to her memory," sneered Valentine.

"She loved me very dearly—at the last," replied Madge sorrowfully.

She stood leaning against the doorpost, in her straight black gown and Puritan cap, while he sat on the bench and lighted his cigar, just as in the old days when he was her lover. But there was no talk of love between them now. A shadow of seriousness rested upon both. In her it was thoughtfulness; in him it was impenetrable gloom.

"The Forlorn Hope," he said. "A queer name for a house. I rather like it though, because it is queer. Was the name your fancy?"

"Yes."

"And you take in fallen women, and nurse them in their last illnesses, and make believe that they are not altogether worthless?"

"They are not worthless—they are those over whom the angels rejoice—they are those who have been lost and are found."

"Ah!" he said listlessly, "you believe in all that. You believe in repentance and the washing of sins. 'Though your sins be as scarlet they shall be white as snow.' I remember hearing that sentence read in church when I was a child. I think the idea of vivid colour in it must have caught my fancy—though they are as scarlet— scarlet—the colour of blood—and of sin—they shall be white—white—white—"

The words dropped slowly from his lips, with a pause after each, dying into silence, as he sat with his head bent, and his eyes upon the ground.

"The Forlorn Hope," he repeated by-and-by, still looking at the ground. "I like the name. Where is your house?"

"In Lisson Grove. I don't suppose you know anything of the neighbourhood."

"Not much; but I have a vague idea of its whereabouts. The Forlorn Hope. Would you take a fallen man if he came to you marked for death? Or do you care only for your own sex?"

"It is for our own sex we have pledged ourselves to work," answered Madge.

"But you would not shut your door against a penitent sinner?"

"I think not—if he were utterly helpless except for us, and we had any power to help him."

"And your mission is to smooth the pillow of

death, and to make the end easy for those who have lived hard and have rioted in sin. Well, I dare say it is a good mission. You are a strange girl, and seem capable of strange things."

He looked at her thoughtfully, admiringly even, but with a grave and respectful admiration which was very different from the young man's sensuous worship of beauty. It was not a lover's gaze which rested on the pale face to-day.

She had aged and altered from the glowing gipsy-like beauty which he had admired in his bachelor days; but she was handsome still, and, while her face had lost in richness of colouring, it had gained in distinction. The lines of the features were more delicate, the ivory tints of the complexion had a more spiritual beauty than the warm carnations of girlhood. She was thinner than she had been then, and looked taller. The straight, tall figure in the straight black gown, the noble head in the Quaker cap, had a grand simplicity which Valentine admired with almost reverent admiration, he in whom reverence for anything was so rare a feeling.

He sat silent, his cigar extinguished, his eyes brooding on the ground again, as he recalled a past which seemed ages away, and the day when he had fancied himself desperately in love with this woman.

He had wooed her passionately, and had tried to win her, yet had wondered at her folly with a contemptuous wonder, when she told him she must be his wife or nothing. He had laughed within himself at the idea that he could be thought capable of marrying a basket-maker's granddaughter, a half-bred gipsy.

He had chosen a mate of his own rank, thoroughbred like himself, penniless as the basket-maker's granddaughter, but a lady by birth and want of education. The girl taught in the National School could have beaten the Colonel's daughter upon any subject on which they could have been examined, from the multiplication table to Early English literature.

And now he asked himself what his life might have been like had he flung conventionality to the winds, made light of caste, and married Mrs.

Maudeville's daughter? Would things have gone as badly with him! Would he have been as careless of her as he had been of Helen, and would some other man have found out that she was fair, and tempted her away from him? Would any man have dared to tempt this woman? Would any fashionable sybarite have ventured to approach this Egyptian sphinx, in silken dalliance, with the light airy courtesies which smooth the brimstone path of seduction? Looking at that grand face, those dark, deep eyes, with their steady outlook, it seemed to him that this woman, once having taken upon herself the vows of a wife, would have kept them until death. It seemed to him, also, that no man who was her husband would have dared to trifle with her happiness.

CHAPTER IV.

"WOULD SHE HAVE TOUCHED MY HAND?"

VALENTINE BELFIELD went back to the marsh next day with his gun and his dogs, shot a brace of birds, and then made his way to the basket-maker's cottage. He was drawn there irresistibly. He wanted to see that earnest face again, to hear those low and steady accents, which fell upon his ear and brain with a soothing influence, like organ music stealing along a vaulted roof to the homeless wanderer lingering by a cathedral door.

There had been more comfort to him in yesterday's conversation with Madge than in anything that had happened to him since the doing of that deed which separated him for ever from his fellow-men. He found himself wondering what would happen if he were to tell her of his crime—if he were to unburden his overloaded breast to this woman whom he had once loved with a selfish sensual love, but whom he now reverenced as a creature of superior mould. He knew not how the change had come about. It might be the consciousness of his own guilt, which intensified his sense of her superiority. Three years ago he had laughed at her pretension to equality as woman against man : and now he longed to hide his weary head in her lap, and to pour out the dark story of his crime. He wanted her compassion, her help against the evil spirit that was rending him.

"If it is her mission to rescue the fallen, she ought to care for me," he thought. "None ever fell lower—none was ever deeper dyed with the stains of sin ! "

The door of old Dawley's cottage was shut, and it was the basket-maker himself who appeared at Valentine's knock.

"How d'ye do, Dawley ? " said Valentine. "I have been shooting about here, and I thought I'd look in upon you. The rheumatism is better, I hope."

"Well, no, sir ; that complaint ain't like good wine. It don't improve with age," answered the old man, not altogether unsuspicious. "Did her ladyship send any message for me or my daughter?"

"No; my mother did not know that I was coming this way. I was surprised to see your daughter here yesterday. She left the Abbey very abruptly three years ago, and I don't think any of our people had heard of her since."

"I beg your pardon, sir, I think Mrs. Marrable had. I believe my girl wrote to her—after her mother's death," answered Dawley, placing a chair for his visitor, and resuming his own seat beside the fire. "I know she must have seemed ungrateful for cutting off from such a good place, and a place in which she had been so kindly treated, without giving proper warning. But she's a strange girl, Mr. Belfield, is my granddaughter, and she thought she had a mission in life, and that that mission was to look after her poor sinful mother; and look after her mother she did, and brought her out of a burning fiery furnace, and cared for her, and worked for her, and nursed her to the end, and buried her—all with the price of her own labour. She worked like a galley-slave, did that girl of mine.   And she did what she wanted to do, and what she thought her duty : which is a good deal more than most of us do."

" Has your daughter been dead long ? "

" Nearly two years.   She was in a decline when Madge found her.   She'd lived like a lady, and drove her own carriage," said the old man, with a touch of pride, " though she'd had her ups and downs."

" I saw her in London four or five years ago," said Valentine, " the remains of a splendid woman."

" She'd spent more money in her time than many a lady born and bred," pursued Dawley, waxing prouder, " and she died a penitent woman, and has gone to glory," he concluded, with pious unction.

" Is this the first time your granddaughter has been to see you since she left the Abbey ? "

" No, she came once before.   She came to tell me of her mother's death.   I wanted her to stop with me altogether then—or to go back to the Abbey, if her ladyship would forgive her and take her back —but she had set her heart upon what she calls her mission, and off she goes again.   She's a good girl to me, all the same. She writes to me once a month, and she sends me a little money now and again. She's gone to see Mr. Rockstone this afternoon, and she's going back to London to-morrow."

"How does she get money to carry on her work in London?"

"All manner of ways. Sometimes by begging, sometimes by the sweat of her brow. She goes out nursing now and again, among people who can afford to pay her handsomely for her services. She learnt how to nurse consumptive patients in attending upon her mother. She had a long lingering illness, had my girl—died by inches, as the saying is—and Madge nursed her through it all. There was a famous doctor that had known something of my girl when she was in her prime, and the tip-top of fashion—and he attended her in her illness, and was kind and generous to her, so that she never wanted for anything. And he took to Madge, and told her she had a genius for nursing—and it was he who recommended her afterwards to his rich patients, and set her going as a sick nurse."

"And in her leisure hours she has founded a sisterhood," interrogated Valentine.

"Yes—and the other sisters are all ladies—ladies, born and bred. There's been some kind of blight upon 'em, one and all—disappointments in their love affairs—or the loss of a relation—or a bad husband. They've all of 'em had their own sorrows before they began to think of other people's troubles. Some of 'em have a little bit of money—some haven't a sixpence—but they all work alike, and most of their money goes to help the poor wretched creatures they take, sick or dying, off the cruel streets of London. It's a good bit of work, Mr. Belfield, for a young woman like my Madge to have done in less than two years."

"Yes, it is a good work—and your grand-daughter is a wonderful woman," said Valentine musingly.

He remembered how lightly he had thought of this girl three years ago, and with what an insolent sense of his own superiority he had approached her, deeming her his predestined prey. And now

he knew that she was, and had always been, infinitely his superior.

He propitiated old Dawley with a gift of money
for future tobacco, and a small supply of his own
tobacco for immediate use ; and then he took up
his hat and prepared to go back to his boat and
his dogs.

" Will you ask Madge to go and see my mother?"
he said. "I think Lady Belfield would like to
hear about her work in Lisson Grove. Ask her
to go to tea at the Abbey to-morrow. I'll tell my
mother to expect her."

" You are very good, sir; but I believe my gal
has made up her mind to go back to London by an
early train to-morrow."

"But a day won't make much difference. Ask
her to put off her journey for a day or two. I
know my mother would like to see her."

It was his own idea, and he had hardly thought
of his mother's mind in the matter. He was feverishly eager that Madge should be encouraged and
helped in her work.

He rowed slowly homeward along the broad

river, keeping close in to the shore. About half a
mile from Dawley's cottage he saw the woman
whose image filled his mind—a tall figure in a
straight black gown, moving with steady pace along
the dusty tow-path. He pulled into the bank,
grounded his boat, and stepped on shore.

"I have just left your grandfather, Madge," he
said. "He has told me all about you." And then
he urged her to go to his mother on the following
afternoon.

"She will be interested in your work, and she
will give you some money," he said; and then he
turned out one of his pockets and gave her a little
heap of gold and silver, amounting to between six
and seven pounds.

"It is not much," he said, "but it is all I have
left of this year's income. No; don't refuse it," as
she made a gesture of repudiation; "I have no need
for money in this place. Don't refuse it unless
you want to wound me."

"Why should I want to wound you?"

"Ah, why, indeed! I once behaved like a cad to
you : but I am not the same man as I was then. I

may be a worse man, perhaps—but anyhow, I am different.   I shall never insult you again, Madge."

"I am sure you will not," she said, looking at him with a compassionate gaze.

She had heard the Chadford people talk of his wife's elopement, and she had been told that Valentine Belfield was a broken man, so altered that his closest friends of the past felt as if he were a stranger among them.   She was sorry for him, and felt herself in some measure responsible for his misery, since it was her anonymous warning which had precipitated his marriage with Helen Deverill.

She took his gift for the Forlorn Hope, and promised to go to the Abbey next day.

"I have been with Mr. Rockstone this afternoon," she said; "he has given me seventeen pounds.   Ten pounds are his own gift, and the rest he has collected among his friends.   I must hurry back to grandfather now, sir," she concluded.   "I have so little time to spend with him.   Good-bye."

"Good-bye, Madge."

He held out his hand, and she took it in frank

friendliness. His clasp was strong and fervent, and he sighed as he released her hand, and then walked on in silence.

" Would she have touched my hand if she knew all ? " he asked himself, as he went back to his boat.

CHAPTER V.

COLONEL DEVERILL loitered in London for a week or so after he left the Abbey.   He put up at a sporting club in Piccadilly, where there were rooms for birds of passage, and he spent his life in a variety of smoking-rooms and billiard-rooms, card-rooms and reading-rooms.   He was a member of seven West-end clubs, and had a choice of places in which to smoke and saunter: but the clubs were nearly empty at this time of the year, and the few men whom he knew were coming and going—full of their autumnal engagements, unsettled and distracted: not in a frame of mind to be good company for a solitary wanderer like the Colonel, who had made no plans for autumn or winter, and who was beginning to feel old and desolate.

The men he knew were civil, and some of them had a sympathetic air, which implied compassion

for him in his affliction as a father; but he felt a
sting even in sympathy, and dreaded lest some
officious friend should offer to condole with him.
He wondered whether his daughter's flight had
become town-talk. There had been no stir made—
no row, or open scandal, and it was possible that her
disgrace was only guessed at by the few who were
behind the scenes of society. There was one man,
however, Sir Randal Greswold, of the County Clare
Rangers, with whom Colonel Deverill was on terms
of almost brotherly confidence and from him he
withheld nothing

"Have you heard anything about that scoundrel,
St. Austell," he asked. "Do people know that he
has gone off with my daughter?"

"Upon my word, Deverill, I don't think anybody
knows as much as that, but I believe there's a
general idea that Mrs. Belfield has gone wrong
somehow. One never can tell how these things
get known. They seem to be in the air. St.
Austell was always about with her, you see.
There was no mistaking the nature of his attentions. The fellow is all the more dangerous,

because there is a vein of sincerity in him; he is desperately in earnest for the time being. People saw that he was over head and ears in love with your daughter; and when he sold his share in the racing stable and announced his intention of going to Ceylon, every one knew what it meant. He was going off with Mrs. Belfield."

"Do you know if—if any one has seen them together?" faltered the Colonel.

"He was seen in Paris—with a lady; he was heard of at Genoa—with a lady; and he was heard of again at Venice—with a lady—only a week ago."

"I have a good mind to go after them, and try to bring her back with me," said Colonel Deverill.

"Don't attempt it, my dear fellow. A father's influence and a father's authority go for nothing against an infatuation of that kind. A little later perhaps, when they are both tired of each other, you may do something, but not now. Besides, they would be on board a P. and O. before you could get to Venice, or they would be hiding somewhere in the Apennines or the Austrian Tyrol."

The Colonel felt the wisdom of this advice. He was not the kind of man to wander all over Europe in search of an erring daughter; though he was assuredly the kind of man to shoot his daughter's seducer, could they two be brought face to face without too much trouble on the Colonel's part. *Laissez faire* had been the rule of his existence. It had left him in very low water in this latter stage of life; but he did not murmur against fate. This last blow hit him harder than any loss of fortune. He went to Wilkie Mansions in search of sympathy from his elder daughter; but Mrs. Baddeley was at Ostend with some friends who had a big yacht—a certain Mr. and Mrs. Digby Smithers, Stock Exchange people, newly rich, and very glad to cultivate the friendship of a lady who went everywhere, or nearly everywhere, and who knew nearly everybody. That there were some people whom Mrs. Baddeley had never succeeded in knowing gave her just that touch of poor humanity which brought her in sympathy with

Mrs. Digby Smithers, who found it hard work to force her way in society, even by the aid of Gunter and Dan Godfrey.   Under these circumstances, Mrs. Digby Smithers' houses in Eaton Place and at Marlow, and Mr. Digby Smithers' yacht, the *Clotho*, were very much at Mrs. Baddeley's service, and still more at the service of Mrs. Baddeley's fashionable friends.

"Ask as many nice fellows as you like," said Smithers. "There are eight good cabins in the *Clotho*, and she's pretty well found, as I think you know."

"The *Clotho* is fairyland," cried Leo gaily. "The *Clotho* ought to be called Fortunatus or the Wishing Cap. One has only to ask and to have. When I had one of my bad headaches the other day, and Mrs. Digby Smithers wrung from me that there was only one brand of champagne that ever did my headaches the least good, there was a bottle of that very brand open beside my berth in two minutes. The *Clotho* is a yacht of miracles. If it were only big enough to carry a roc's egg, I should not scruple to ask for one. I know it would be there. Perhaps you have some patent compressible rocs' eggs in the hold at this very moment."

Digby Smithers laughed. He liked Mrs. Baddeley to chaff him about his yacht, though he did not always follow her meaning. He was not a man of profound reading. He had, in fact, never read anything except the newspapers, and there his studies were confined to such information as affected his own interests. For thirty years of his life—from seventeen to forty-seven—he had given himself up to the business of money-making: and now at forty-seven he had at last brought himself to believe that he had made enough money and could afford to spend some. Hitherto his wife and he had been content to live their jogtrot lives in Bloomsbury, at an expenditure of seven hundred a year, taking their chief pleasure from the knowledge that they were putting a good many thousands behind them as they jogged along; but at last the time had come when Mrs. Smithers, childless, and seeing her charms on the wane, told herself, and told her husband, that it was now or never. If they were ever to see life and enjoy the fruits of prosperity, there was not an hour to lose.

Urged by his wife, therefore, Mr. Smithers assumed the prenomen Digby, bestowed on him in baptism by an impecunious half-pay captain, with whom Smithers the elder had claimed cousinship. With an almost feverish haste he exchanged Bloomsbury for Eaton Place, and the philistine upholstery of Finsbury for the artistic cabinet work and high art fabrics of Druce. He bought a river-side villa at Marlow, and a steam-launch, which speedily became a horror to rowing men; but Mrs. Smithers, who hankered for a life of excitement, found the steam-launch dull, and insisted upon a two-hundred-ton yacht.

Mrs. Baddeley had made this worthy couple's acquaintance at Marlow, where their villa was used as a water-side hotel by a somewhat rowdy social circle, and where the luncheon table was openly talked of as the table d'hôte. Leo and her chosen friends used the table d'hôte freely, made undisguised fun of the Smitherses, and found fault with their cook; but anything had been forgiven in a lady who had two or three tame noblemen in her train, first among all, Lord St. Austell, whose reputation as a man of fashion seemed all the better because of its savour of iniquity. No virtuous nobleman had ever achieved such world-wide renown as the erring St. Austell.

Colonel Deverill went over to Ostend, to confer with his elder daughter, and was received on board the *Clotho* with oppressive cordiality.

" You will stay, of course, Colonel," said Digby Smithers, who was a short stout man, pink of complexion and sandy of hair; " you shall have one of our best cabins—the one we saved for St. Austell. He promised us a week in September, but those troublesome doctors have sent him off to the East."

The Colonel spent a couple of nights on board, in the cabin that was to have been St. Austell's. He only stayed those two nights in order to have a quiet talk with his daughter.

Mrs. Baddeley was looking ill, and was obviously

out of spirits, though she put on an air of forced gaiety now and then out of compliment to her hostess. Even Tory's blandishments seemed to have lost their charm, and she allowed that sagacious animal's somewhat fickle fancy to be won by Mrs. Digby Smithers, who had conceived an ardent affection for him, and who ministered to his appetite with a reckless disregard of consequences.

"You look dreadfully cut up, Leo," said her father, when they were sitting together under an awning, at a comfortable distance from Mrs. Digby Smithers and a brace of frisky matrons, all absorbed by the fascinations of Tory, and all diversifying the inanity of their conversation by still more inane gigglings.

"I am dreadfully cut up," she answered curtly.

"Well, I don't wonder at it. The girl was in your charge, and you must have felt responsible for her in some measure. I suppose there's no doubt she went off with St. Austell—and not with any other man?"

" Doubt ? If you had seen them together, you would not ask such a question."

" But if you saw how things were tending, why didn't you stop her—you are ever so much older—and a woman of experience ? "

" Stop her ! Could you stop the Ganges ? She went headlong to destruction from the hour he began to care for her. You don't know what he is when he pretends to be in love with a woman ! God knows what he is when he is really in love : and I suppose he was really in love with Helen."

The Colonel listened with a thoughtful brow.

" It's a bad business," he said, " and I don't see any remedy for it. If he were only free—but I suppose there is no hope that his wife will take it into her head to divorce him——"

" She can't do it, if she would. Her own position won't bear scrutiny. He might have divorced her five years ago if he had chosen : but he didn't choose. There were money interests at stake ; and I think he preferred his own position, as a married man without the incumbrance of a wife, to absolute freedom. He might trifle with any woman's affections and not fear to be called to account, don't you know. And to an unprincipled man the position has its advantages."

"I wish he had been free to make your sister an honest woman," said the Colonel gloomily.

"You mean free to make her Lady St. Austell," sneered Leo. "If she had run away with a Jones or a Smith, you would not care half so much about her honesty. I know your Irish pride."

"Can I help having kings for my ancestors? A feeling of that kind is in a man's blood. Do you know where Lady St. Austell is and what she is doing?"

"She is at Naples, I believe—she has a villa somewhere in the suburbs, and lives in a certain style. She has a rich Italian Marquis for her banker, and is said to spend money rather recklessly. I am told she takes chloral; so there might be a chance for Helen, if St. Austell doesn't get tired of her too soon."

"How heartlessly you talk of your sister."

"She has ceased to be my sister. I have done with her for ever."

"One would think you had been in love with St. Austell, or you would hardly be so bitter."

"Suppose I was in love with him! At any rate, I did not compromise myself on his account. Why could not Helen take care of herself as I have done? Could she not like a man—without throwing herself into his arms?"

"She was less a woman of the world than you, Leonora. It is not every woman who can take care of herself as you have done, and yet amuse herself as you do."

A month later, Colonel Deverill opened his *Times,* on board his Scotch friends' yacht in the Orkneys, and started at seeing a line in large type, among the telegraphic news : "Cholera at Naples. Seventeen deaths."

"By Jove!" muttered the Colonel, with a thrill of guilty hope, "Lady St. Austell will have to cut and run from her Neapolitan villa."

Would she cut and run? Hardly, unless she were a very foolish woman. Dire diseases which ravage the slums and cellars of a city, the lanes and alleys and crowded quarters where the poor congregate, are rarely known to visit suburban villas perched high on the crest of a flower-scented hill, with their backs to the orange groves and their faces to the sea. No cholera poison would pollute the air that blew in at Lady St. Austell's windows. She would be safe enough.

Notwithstanding this opinion that no harm could possibly come to Lady St. Austell, Colonel Deverill read the cholera column with a keener interest than other parts of the paper, and had a particularly sharp eye for news from Naples. Cholera was reported all through Southern Italy, as well as at Toulon and Marseilles; and every day showed a new list of victims. All the English visitors were leaving Naples and its vicinity.

At last appeared the name for which Colonel Deverill was on the watch.

"Lady St. Austell has left her villa at Posilipo for the island of Capri, where she will be the guest of the Marchese of Lugarno di Melina, whose picturesque chateau and orange groves are known to Italian tourists. No case of cholera has been heard of on the island."

"So she has cut and run after all," said the Colonel. "What nervous fools some women are! And yet they are of the same clay as Florence Nightingale and her sisterhood."

After this the Colonel glanced at the cholera news with a careless eye. The one woman, whose death might have seemed a special favour of providence, was out of reach of infection—safe on her sea-girt isle.

Colonel Deverill unfolded his *Galignani* one wintry morning in Paris, some weeks after he had forgotten all about Naples and the cholera, and this time he was startled much more seriously than by the Neapolitan news of September.

"We regret to announce the death of Lady St. Austell, who expired at Les Orangers, Capri, after a long illness. Her ladyship was among the English residents who fled from Naples at the first outbreak of cholera; and, from the time of her flight, she had been suffering from a nervous fever, which ended fatally on Saturday morning.

Lady St. Austell was the seventh daughter of the Earl of Swathling."

" Gone!" cried the Colonel. " Then there will be a chance for my girl, after all."

To raise his daughter from disgrace and seclusion to a better place in the world than that which she had occupied before her fall was the strongest desire of Colonel Deverill's mind. He hardly stopped to ask himself whether society would accept such a marriage as a rehabilitation; whether the world would ever consent to condone the past; whether the divorced Mrs. Belfield would be forgotten in the second Lady St. Austell. The one point in his mind was that reparation could now be made to his daughter, and that it was his business to bring her seducer to book.

The first thing to be managed, however, would be the divorce; and that must needs be a work of time and of unpleasantness. It must be brought about with the least possible publicity, and it would be the Colonel's duty to use all the influence he could command, in order to shorten those loathsome reports which are sport to the newspaper reader, and death to those whose names figure therein. Colonel Deverill had been daily expecting to hear that his son-in-law had petitioned for a divorce; but he had as yet received no notice to that effect. The young man was evidently in no haste to free himself; but now he would have to be gently stimulated to the effort. With a man of St. Austell's temperament there was no time to be lost. He must not be allowed to tire of his latest victim before he was free to espouse her.

He felt that the matter was one in which he could not afford to be precipitate. He must approach the question delicately, in the character of a disinterested friend and broken-hearted father. With this view, he wrote to Lady Belfield, asking her to hire the furnished cottage on the bank of the Chad for him, if it were still in the market.

"I am tired of Paris, and I don't care for another winter on the Riviera," he wrote. "I spent two seasons at Nice with my girls, when life was brighter with me than it is now. Those scenes would only awaken painful associations. Your Devonshire climate is mild enough for a tough old soldier like me—so if you can get the cottage for me on reasonable terms I will engage it for six months, and telegraph to my butler and his wife to take possession."

Lady Belfield replied by telegram. "Cottage taken. Feel sure you will approve terms."

"Admirable woman," replied the Colonel; "as business-like as she is charming. If my poor girl had married the right brother instead of the wrong one, how happy we might have been."

He made all his arrangements, and was established in Myrtle Cottage within ten days of that announcement in *Galignani*. The slovenly old Irish butler and the slammerkin Irish housekeeper had the art of making their master comfortable. A red-elbowed drudge, hired in the neighbourhood, and a boy to clean boots, run errands, and work in the garden, completed the household, and the Colonel was more carefully ministered to than many a man with thirty or forty servants.

The cottage was picturesque without being damp—an admirable quality in cottages. It stood well above the river, with about an acre of garden sprawling in an irregular figure on the hillside—good old garden ground, teeming with old-fashioned perennials, and rich in old-fashioned shrubs, guelder roses, golden broom, arbutus, lilac, and laburnum. The rooms were small, cosy—furnished with substantial furniture of the Reform Bill era—clumsy, ponderous, comfortable. Lady Belfield had taken a basket of hot-house flowers to fill all the bowls and vases, had seen cheery wood fires lighted in all the rooms, and had spread new magazines and periodicals on a table in the drawing-room, so that the Colonel's first exclamation on entering the room was: "This looks like home."

There was a note from Lady Belfield on the chimney-piece, asking him to dinner that evening, which he hastened to accept by means of a hurried scrawl and the handy boy. There was no one at the Abbey but the family, and the dinner was not lively, although Constance Belfield did all in her power to maintain the interest of the conversation. There was a dogged gloom in Valentine's manner which repelled confidence, and there was a subdued melancholy upon Adrian's countenance, which was only brightened when he addressed his mother.

"Val has had one of his long days with the fox-hounds," said Lady Belfield apologetically, "so you must not take any notice of him if he is dull."

Colonel Deverill was bent upon conciliating his son-in-law, and was careful to talk of the things Valentine loved. They played a couple of games at billiards after dinner, and talked of the hunting. Valentine was gloomy, but not ill-natured.

"If you care about hunting, we can mount you for two days a week all through the season," he said. "There are plenty of good hunters. My mother has been very generous to me lately, and we have increased the stud. It is the only thing a man can do in this gloomy hole."

"You find Chadford gloomy."

"I always did. I have tolerated the place because it is my home—it has been needs must, don't you know—but I believe I have always hated it. I'm very sure I hate it now."

This seemed natural in a man who had been badly treated. The Colonel paused upon his stroke to sigh, and then made his cannon neatly, with a subdued air.

"You have had reason to dislike the place—lately," he said despondently, and then he dawdled for a little, as he chalked his cue, trying to find the best words in which to approach a risky subject. "You—you have not petitioned for your divorce yet, I suppose."

He said *your* divorce, making the matter, as it were, a foregone conclusion, and in his son-in-law's especial interest.

"I am not going to petition," answered Valentine.

The Colonel tried an impossible cannon off the red in sheer confusion of mind.

"Not going to petition!" he faltered.

"No. Why should I? I don't want to marry again—I never should marry again—whatever might occur. I have made one mistake, and I had rather abide by it."

"My dear Valentine, that is one way of looking at the matter. Forgive me if I say it's not the right way."

" Where's the wrong ? "

" To yourself first—to my wretched daughter in the second place.   You don't want to marry again you say—of course you don't—not now.   Your wound is too raw yet; every touch is agony. Wait till your wound is healed, my dear boy—and fancy yourself then thrown into the society of a pretty and sympathetic woman—who pities you, and is quite ready to give you a happier experience of married life.   Get your divorce, and you may let the coming years do what they like for you—find you a wife or not, as Heaven may order. But keep yourself bound to a woman who has been false to you, and you shut yourself out from all hope of future consolation."

" I am not the kind of man to be consoled—in that way," answered Valentine doggedly, going on playing as he talked.   " I would rather bear my burden in my own manner, if you please, Colonel Deverill.   I don't complain of anybody, and I don't ask anybody for consolation—that's game, I think—or for advice."

" So be it.   Then we'll leave you out of the

question," said the Colonel, putting his cue in the rack, with an air of imperturbable good temper. "But now we have to think of my daughter. I have her interests very much at heart, Mr. Belfield, although I grant you she has behaved deuced badly; and her interests demand a divorce without loss of time."

"What! You really want to see your daughter in the Divorce Court, to have her name bandied about in every newspaper in the kingdom!"

"I want to see her righted by the man who has led her wrong," answered the Colonel. "I want to see her Lord St. Austell's wife before these grey hairs go down in sorrow to the grave."

"Lord St. Austell's wife!" cried Valentine, with an hysterical laugh. "Oh, I see your game, Colonel. Lady St. Austell died a week or two ago, and St. Austell is free to marry again—and you would like him to marry your daughter. You are a far-seeing man, upon my soul."

He burst out laughing—laughed long and loud this time; but it was the laugh of hysteria and not of mirth. His face had whitened gradually since the beginning of this conversation, and he now looked ghastly as he stood leaning against the billiard table in the glare of the lamps. Presently the laugh changed to a choking cough, and he put his handkerchief suddenly to his lips. When he took it away a minute afterwards, the Colonel noticed crimson stains upon the white cambric.

"Do you spit blood?" he asked.

"Occasionally. It is nothing of any consequence."

"That is a question for your doctor to decide. I don't like to hear a powerfully-built young man hysterical, or to see him spit blood."

There was a silence for some minutes, while each man lighted a cigarette.

"Has my daughter sent for her luggage yet?"

"No."

"Strange."

"Very strange. Will you come to the drawing-room and have a chat with my mother?"

"I think not. It's getting late, so I won't disturb her. I'm going to walk home."

They went into the hall together, and Valentine

helped the Colonel on with his overcoat. When they shook hands, Colonel Deverill noticed that the young man's hand was cold and damp.

"There is something wrong with my son-in-law," he said to himself, as he walked across the park, on his way to a small private gate which opened into a lane behind his cottage; "and it's deuced awkward that he should put up his back against a divorce. I believe it is sheer malevolence towards my unhappy daughter. There are some men who don't know how to be generous."

Although the Colonel was very fond of a good run with the hounds, he did not take advantage of Valentine's offer of a mount. He went the round of the stables with Sir Adrian one non-hunting morning, and examined all the horses, and praised some of them; but he would not put himself under an obligation to his son-in-law.

"I don't feel like hunting this winter, for I've had some ugly twitches of gout," he said; "I shall wait for a little fishing in the spring, or I may have a shot at the birds on the marshes—with your permission, Sir Adrian. I think your land ruus down as far as the basket-maker's cottage."

"And for nearly a mile beyond," replied Adrian.

Lady Belfield begged Colonel Deverill to drop in at the Abbey whenever he liked. She felt very sorry for him in his solitude; and she felt also that Valentine owed him some amends for the evil end that had come to his daughter's married life. It had not been all Helen's fault. The husband's neglect had to be counted as well as the wife's folly.

The Colonel settled himself in his new quarters, and was content for some weeks to lead a sleepy kind of life—shooting a little, walking a little, reading the newspapers, and dozing by his solitary fireside of an evening after his solitary dinner. He was heavy at heart in spite of all outward signs of contentment. He knew that he had not been a careful father, and that the burden of his daughter's sin must rest in some part upon his conscience. All the paternal affection of which he was capable had been awakened by his daughter in her hour of disgrace. He had thought of her and cared for her very little in her early married life, deeming that it was her husband's business to take care of her; but now in his rustic solitude her image haunted him perpetually, and his soul was sorely troubled for her sake.

" If I could but see her Lady St. Austell before I die, I might go down to the grave in peace," he said to himself.

He had dreams about her in his cottage bed-chamber, lulled by the plish-plash of the flowing tide. His sleep was haunted by those distorted visions, in which a vague reflection of our waking anxieties is interwoven with the nonsense-pictures of sleep. He saw her standing at the altar with St. Austell by her side; but there was always some discordant image, something to stop the ceremony before the vows were spoken—or St. Austell changed into some incongruous stranger—or the church was not a church—or the parson was not a parson. No such dream ever came to a happy ending—and he dreamt such dreams by the score.

" I shall go off my head if I lead this lonely life much longer," he told himself, waking in the dead of night after one of those troubled visions. "I must get Leonora to stay with me."

He telegraphed to Mrs. Baddeley next morning—

"Dull, despondent, and ill. For God's sake come and take care of me."

Mrs. Baddeley was far from being perfect; but she was not a Goneril, and she arrived by the express next day, with her Russian poodle.

CHAPTER VI.

TORY was in high health and spirits, his thorough-bred back shorn with modish severity, and his tufts arranged after the latest fashion. His Indian bangles jingled as he walked at his mistress's side, and his neck ribbon was of the new colour. There is always a new colour, known only to the *élite*. No sooner does it become known to the external world than it ceases to be the mode.

Tory's mistress was not looking her best. She had lost her brilliant carnation, and the splendour of her Irish eyes was dim. She looked five years older than when her father had seen her at the beginning of the last London season.

"My dear Leo, you look ill and worried," said the Colonel, as they drove away from the station, Tory sitting on the seat opposite them, shivering in his little cloth overcoat, trimmed with Astrachan, and looking about him with his topaz eyes as if he did not admire the country.

"How can I help it? Of course I have been worried," answered Leo discontentedly. "Do you suppose I have not felt the disgrace of Helen's conduct?"

"Is it generally known, do you think?"

"People know there is something wrong. Valentine ordered everything to be sold off about a month ago—all those pretty Japanese things, which I took an infinitude of trouble to get for them. They went for a mere song. I made Beeching buy a good many lots for me—screens and vases, and portières—anything I, could find room for. Of course people have talked—and I have been pumped perpetually about her. But it is an odd thing that I have never met with anybody who positively knows that she is with St. Austell. It is strange that no one should have met them abroad."

"I suppose they have been very careful."

"Yes; they certainly must have avoided the beaten tracks. I have watched for paragraphs in *Galignani* or the society papers, and I have cut out half a dozen little allusions to St. Austell, but not one hint about her."

" She must be with him," said the Colonel. " I showed you his letter—the letter I found in her dressing-bag—when we were on board the *Clotho*. That seems decisive."

" Yes, she must be with him," replied Leo, but not with conviction.

She remembered St. Austell's preternatural *sang froid* when she accused him of running away with her sister. She remembered how he had left Charing Cross.

" I will show you the paragraphs when I can get at my despatch-box," she said. " And now tell me all about yourself. Why did you return to this dull neighbourhood, with its wretched associations ? "

" Because I had a good deal to say to my son-in-law. Now that St. Austell is a free man, there ought to be no time lost in getting a divorce, don't you know ? "

" In order that he may marry Helen," cried Leo, as if she had been stung.

"Of course. It is the only thing that can set her right."

"And do you think he would marry her if she were free to-morrow?" Leo asked contemptuously. "Do you know Lord St. Austell so little as to suppose that he would burden himself with a wife when he has secured a mistress—a mistress whose attractions must have grown stale by this time—a mistress who, no doubt, has made the one grand mistake that all women make under such circumstances, and has bored him with tears and contrition. A divorce will only advertize her disgrace. It will not bring her any nearer marriage with St. Austell."

"Let me once see her free to marry, and St. Austell shall make her his wife, or account to me for her dishonour," said the Colonel fiercely.

"He won't refuse to meet you. He is a crack shot like yourself—perhaps in much better practice. He will give you satisfaction, I dare say—but he won't marry my sister."

"You are diabolically bitter against that poor

girl, Leonora, and I must say I think it very un-womanly on your part."

"Ah, but you see women look at these things from a different standpoint. With you men a woman has only to go wrong in order to become interesting. You open your arms to her, are ready to shelter her and fight for her. For a woman to be very pretty, and to go astray in the first bloom of her prettiness, is to command your chivalrous service. Women had need be cruel to each other, or vice would be at too high a premium."

The Colonel was distressed at his daughter's tone, but he was very glad to have her society all the same. Her presence brightened the cottage, and put flight for the time being to those morbid fancies which were beginning to weigh heavily on the Colonel—the fancy that his daughter was ill and dying in a far-off land, that St. Austell might ill-treat or desert her. Even Tory was an acquisition, and the sight of that intellectual animal, sitting bolt upright on the hearthrug, with his mouth open, and his yellow eye-balls glaring at the fire, helped to raise Colonel Deverill's drooping spirits. The Gladstonian performance with a lump of sugar might pall, if repeated more than twenty times a day—nor was it all rapture to hear Tory play " God Save the Queen " upon a damp cottage piano—but there was usefulness in a dog that rushed at every open door, and shut it with a cheerful bang. Even Tory's dinner made a little diversion in the long winter evening, and afforded a topic for conversation.

Mrs. Baddeley did her best to cheer her father, but she was evidently out of spirits, and the effort to appear lively was almost beyond her strength. Her own affairs were not free from entanglement; for in spite of the devoted Beeching's aid—given on many occasions, as in the dressmaker difficulty —she was considerably in debt. She had not forgotten that she had a husband in India; and while he remained there he had been eminently useful to her as a shield against the shafts of slander, and an invisible court of appeal. When asked by her admirers to join in any risky adventure—a little dinner that verged on the disreputable—a water picnic in doubtful society—she had always been able to decline gracefully on the plea that she had a husband in India.

"I think you know I am not a prude," she would say; "and I admire that lovely Mrs. Rochejaquelin Green beyond measure; but I don't think Frank would *quite* like me to meet her *en petit comité*. One cannot avoid being friendly afterwards, you see. I should be pestered with cards for her parties, and Frank might be angry."

But now Frank's regiment was to return to England in the following March, and Frank would be no longer a dear fellow in India, useful to be referred to on all occasions, but by no means troublesome or inquisitive. He would come home; and his arrival would be the signal for clamorous tradespeople to push their demands. His welcome to the nest in South Kensington would be a shower of bills, lawyers' letters, and county court summonses.

"I'm afraid poor Frank will have to go through the Bankruptcy Court," mused Mrs. Baddeley, with a compassionate sigh. "I hope he won't much mind. A good many people do it nowadays—quite nice people; and society seems to think very little the worse of them. Short of being inordinately rich, money doesn't count in society."

Reasoning thus, the fair Leonora told herself she had no cause for being down-hearted; yet in the picturesque seclusion of Myrtle Cottage her spirits sank, and the prospect of future difficulties grew daily darker. She had hitherto lived the kind of life in which there is no leisure for thought; and now all at once she found herself with nothing to do but read novels and think of her own affairs. The novels were for the most part less interesting than her own embarrassments, and they failed to distract her. The quiet beauty of her surroundings, the broad river, the wooded hills in the foreground and the dark ridge of the moor beyond, had no charm for her.

"It is a cut-throat place!" she exclaimed, with a shiver.

The Colonel and his daughter dined at the

Abbey on Christmas Day. It was a green Christmas, mild, misty, depressing. Leo wore one of her loveliest gowns—an arrangement of dark red velvet with glittering ruby beads, which made a glowing atmosphere about her, and suggested cheerfulness; but nobody was honestly and unaffectedly cheerful at that small Christmas dinner. Mr. Rockstone made the bravest effort at mirthfulness, and filled up every gap in the conversation; but there was a gloom upon Valentine's face which would have spread a dulness in the most convivial circle, and Colonel Deverill was obviously depressed. His dreams had been troubled on the previous night. Shapeless visions had disturbed his slumbers, and filled his mind with gloom. He was weighed down by formless apprehensions. He could not define to himself what it was that he dreaded. He only knew that his mind was full of fear.

"I think I must give up going to the Abbey," he told his daughter as they drove home. "Lady Belfield is charming, and Sir Adrian is as good as gold; but I cannot get on with

Valentine. I'm afraid I'm beginning to hate him."

"That is rather hard upon him," answered Leo, "for he certainly is more sinned against than sinning."

" He was a neglectful husband."

" True; but he was very good-natured. Helen could go where she liked, and enjoy herself as much as she chose. If she had had only common prudence she could have got on very well indeed."

In his retirement at Myrtle Cottage, Colonel Deverill waited for the post which brought him his letters and his newspapers with a keener impatience than he had ever felt before for those luxuries of modern life. On board a friend's yacht, or at any sleepy little Swiss or German water-cure settlement, he had been content to let his days slip by, and to know no more of the outer world than was revealed to him by an occasional *Morning News* or *Galignani*; content to forget the days of the week, and to be surprised by church bells on a Sunday morning; content almost to forget which party was in and which was out, whether his country was drifting to ruin under a Radical Cabinet, or being guided to glory by Conservatives. Letters, he had told himself, were always more likely to bring him worry than pleasure, and, unless he was expecting a cheque from his Irish agent, he was apt to be indifferent to the going and coming of the post.

But now he was intently expectant of every mail, and had a blank and dispirited feeling when the hour was over. He was expecting some kind of communication from his runaway daughter—a letter of penitence—of intercession—a letter of filial love, telling him that he was not forgotten, that even in her sinful life she was still his daughter. He had been expecting such a letter for months, and his heart sickened as the new year began without bringing him one line of greeting from the lost one.

"I suppose she is afraid to address me," he thought. "And yet she ought not to be afraid. I was never severe to my children."

He had a permanent address in London, under

cover to a solicitor's firm in the City, where all letters were re-addressed to him, and this address was known to Helen. She would have had no difficulty in writing to him had she been disposed to write.

The new year began sadly under these circumstances, and even Tory's blandishments could not maintain cheerfulness. Mrs. Baddeley yawned over her novel beside the wood fire, which was the only cheerful thing in the house.

Early in the year there came a budget from Frank Baddeley, which his wife read with good-humoured indifference—till she came to a passage at which her cheek suddenly paled, and her whole aspect changed.

"What is that?" asked the Colonel excitedly, "anything about *her*?"

"No; but it is something about him."

"Read it—read it, please," gasped her father, stretching his hand across the breakfast table, as if to clutch the flimsy sheet.

"Yes. Don't agitate yourself, father. There is not much in it. Frank says, "St. Austell is in

Ceylon. He has been there more than a month, living very quietly, and alone. I have that fact from the best authority, so you must be wrong in your idea that Helen went to Ceylon with him. They may have been together in Italy, as you say, but he arrived at Colombo alone. Tom MacDonald, of the Punjaub Regiment, was there when he came. Perhaps your sister went off with some one else after all, and you are on a false scent."

"Great God!" cried Colonel Deverill, starting up from the breakfast-table, and walking about the room with a distracted air. "What does it all mean? If she is not in Ceylon, where is she? We know that she ran away with St. Austell. There is his letter to prove it."

"She may have changed her mind at the last," said Leo, looking straight before her with a troubled brow, for even to her careless temperament the matter began to assume a mysterious aspect. "Her conscience may have been awakened, and she may have run away from him, and not with him. She may have gone into a convent—or joined some Anglican sisterhood. Who can tell?"

"What am I to do?" groaned the Colonel.

"You might advertize—put an advertisement in the *Times*, so worded that she alone would understand it. Let it be repeated twenty times, at certain intervals, so that if she is in any place where the *Times* circulates, she must eventually see your advertisement."

"How can I advertize so that she will be the only one to understand?"

"Oh, we must invent a code. We must recall something in the past—known to us only—some pet name. Don't you remember, you once used to call her Pansy. She would know that Pansy was meant for her."

Leo took out her pencil, and wrote upon Major Baddeley's envelope. "Pansy's sorrowful father entreats her to write to him. A father's heart can forgive everything. She has a home still with him. Kilrush." She read this rough draft to her father.

"She could not fail to understand that," she

said. "Those two names, Pansy and Kilrush, would be unmistakable."

"Yes, I think she would understand," replied the Colonel. "There are not many people who could write from Kilrush. You are right, Leo. I'll send the advertisement to the *Times* by the next post—with a cheque. I suppose that is a kind of thing one must pay for in advance."

The advertisement appeared at the head of the second column three days later, and the Colonel contemplated it with tears in his eyes. He could fancy his daughter reading it in her seclusion or desolation. Since he had discovered that she was not with St. Austell, he knew not how to picture her to himself: whether deserted and penitent; or whether as a woman who had drawn back upon the brink of the precipice, and had fled from her tempter. All his hopes for her had been dashed by that letter from Major Baddeley. As a father, he had wept over her folly and her sin; but as a man of the world it had seemed to him a good thing that she should become Lady St. Austell. He felt that from a society point of view her reputation was gone for ever, and that her only chance was to dare society in a new character. As a peeress, and a beauty, she might yet become the centre of a brilliant circle—on the Continent.

The advertisement appeared time after time, week after week, until the twentieth insertion had run out, and the Colonel's cheque was exhausted. There had been no reply. The year was two months old, and the spring flowers were blooming in the shrubbery borders at Myrtle Cottage, and the little lawn was gay with golden crocus-cups, and there had been no sign or token from Helen.

Mrs. Baddeley stayed on with her father, though the London season was beginning. It was not that she loved Devonshire more, but that she feared South Kensington most. The tradespeople were pushing for their accounts, and lawyers' letters were growing frequent. It was easier to face these things at a distance than on the spot, where every vibration of the electric bell jarred her nerves, and set her heart beating vehemently, in apprehension of immediate evil. Here at least, though she received the letters, she did not hear the bell; and she was out of reach of any importunate creditor, who might be so audacious as to demand an interview. So she put her arms round the Colonel's neck one morning at breakfast, and told him she would not desert him. She would stay till Frank's return.

"God bless you, my love," faltered her father, "I thought you would stand by me in my loneliness. Indeed, Leo, I am half broken-hearted about your sister. Her present existence is a mystery to me, and I can scarcely bear my life under the burden of that mystery. If she was anywhere within the reach of this paper," striking his fist upon the *Times* which lay open on the table, "she must have understood my appeal. Where in heaven's name is she hiding? Some one must know."

"Yes, some one must know," answered Leonora. "I will tell you of one thing that you can do, father. You cannot go to Ceylon. The journey is too long, and you are too old. But you can telegraph a question to St. Austell. Ask him if he knows where Helen is to be found. Ask him to answer you on his honour. He cannot refuse to answer such an appeal."

" I'll telegraph to him. You are right, Leo. I must find out where my poor girl is. I must leave no stone unturned."

He did not like to send his ocean-message from Chadford Post-office, where it would inevitably give occasion for gossip; so he went to Exeter next day, intending to send the message from there; but, after he had alighted at the Exeter Station, it suddenly occurred to him that he was just in time for the London express, and, on the spur of the moment, he decided on going to London. He telegraphed to Mrs. Baddeley, promising to return next day, and he took his ticket for Waterloo.

It was six o'clock when he arrived, and dark, so he put himself in a hansom, drove straight to the Badminton, and went into the coffee-room to order his dinner. When he had given the order for half-past seven, he went to the reading-room, and seated himself at the table near the fire, to compose his message.

There were telegraph forms on the table, but he began a rough draft on a sheet of paper.

" To Lord St. Austell, Ceylon.

" I entreat you inform me of my daughter's present whereabouts. Answer frankly on your honour, to a heart-broken father. Deverill."

He read the words three times over; wondering if they were strong enough. He paused after the third reading, wiped his forehead with a weary air, and, looking up absently, with his pen in his hand, saw St. Austell standing in front of the fire-place opposite him.

" My God ! " he cried, starting to his feet. " This is the most extraordinary thing. I thought you were in Ceylon."

" I was until a few weeks ago. I came home the week before last—too soon, my doctor tells me, but I was heartily sick of the place. You don't look over well, Deverill."

The Colonel was ghastly. He had dropped back into his seat, and was arranging the papers before him with tremulous fingers.

He handed St. Austell the rough draft of the message, without a word.

"What does it mean?" St. Austell asked, after he had read the blurred words in the Colonel's big penmanship.

"The question is plain enough, I think. Until very lately I thought my daughter was with you in Ceylon. I hear she was not there; but all the same you are likely to know her present address. For pity's sake tell me where she is—at once. I am longing to find her—to protect and cherish her. I am ready to forgive all—to forgive her and you."

The room was empty, but the Colonel spoke in suppressed tones, with the consciousness that he was in a public place.

"My dear Colonel, I wish I could help you—but I can't. As for forgiveness, you have nothing to pardon in me except the fact that I was madly in love with your daughter—and tried to win her— and failed. If my sin in so trying was great, my punishment was greater. I never loved any woman as I loved Helen Belfield, and she threw me over at the last moment."

"But I have your letter of instructions about her journey—everything must have been planned between you."

"It was, so far as I could plan; but I tell you she threw me over. She was to have met me at Exeter, but she didn't. I waited for three trains, and then went on to London in a rage—mad, despairing. I had been most completely fooled."

"But she meant to run away with you?"

"So I thought on the previous afternoon."

"She made her plans deliberately; her trunks were all packed."

"Indeed. That looks business-like. And yet she threw me over, you see, and carried her trunks somewhere else."

"No. Her luggage was all left in her own rooms at the Abbey. Wherever she went, she must have fled from the house in such a state of mind that she took no trouble to secure her own property; nor even her comforts for the journey. Her travelling-bag—my own wedding gift—was left. It was in an inner pocket of that bag that I found your letter."

"And she has not claimed her belongings since then?" asked St. Austell, with a troubled brow.

"No."

"And you have heard nothing of her since that time—absolutely nothing?"

"Not one word. I thought she was with you. You were heard of in Paris—with a lady."

"A passing acquaintance—and a Parisienne."

"You were heard of in Venice—again with a lady."

"An old friend—a Florentine Countess, who was good enough to go about with me a little in my solitude—we dined together, and lunched together *al fresco*, half a dozen times. That was all. And you have heard nothing about your daughter—in all these months—from August to March—you have had no letter from her—no information? directly or indirectly?"

"Not one word."

"Then, Colonel Deverill, I can only say the business looks very alarming," said St. Austell, turning his face to the mantel-piece, and resting his head upon his arm.

The Colonel saw that he was deeply moved. There was a silence of some moments, and then the older man asked in a faltering voice:

"What is it that you fear?"

"I don't know. I—I—can't tell you. My fears are vague and shapeless; but it is a shock to me to find you are so completely in the dark about her. I loved her devotedly, Colonel Deverill. If she had trusted herself to me as she promised, I would have made her my wife, now that I am a free man. I would have done all that a man can do to recompense her for her sacrifice."

"I believe she must be in hiding somewhere; in some Anglican sisterhood, some semi-monastic retreat, where she is not allowed to see the newspapers, or to hold any communication with the outer world," said the Colonel, after a pause.

"Yes, it may be so," answered St. Austell, moving away from the mantel-piece, and seating himself opposite Colonel Deverill at the writing-table. "It may be so. It would be like her to go and bury herself alive in a fit of religious enthusiasm. She was a creature of rapid changes of mood. When I thought I was most secure of her, knowing very well that she loved me, she spread her wings as suddenly as a butterfly, and was gone. I was hardly surprised when she cheated me; but I was very angry. My pride was wounded. I had grovelled before her, and I told myself I would grovel no more. So I went off to the Continent in sullen despair, and I went to Ceylon in the same temper, and my life was loathsome to me all the time I stayed there."

"Upon my soul I am sorry for you," said the Colonel, " though I suppose I ought to be the last man in the world to say so. It is a most unhappy business, unhappy from first to last. She might have married an excellent young man, who could have given her a fine position. She chose to jilt him for the sake of his worthless brother, who neglected her. Her whole life has been a mistake."

"Which she is trying to atone for, perhaps, in the dull round of conventual work, nursing the sick, feeding the hungry, praying, fasting, wearing out her young life within four walls. It is maddening to contemplate," said St. Austell.

And yet it was not so bad as the fear which had shaken him just now, when he had disguised his thought from the Colonel, not daring to breathe that apprehension in a father's ear.

He had feared that Helen might have made away with herself. That she had felt herself too weak to withstand temptation, and had preferred death to dishonour. There might be a woman left, perhaps even in this waning nineteenth century, capable of such a choice.

" Will you let me help you to search for her," he asked, " not directly, but indirectly ? "

" How can you help me ? "

St. Austell took out his card-case, and wrote a name and address on the back of a card.

" That man can help you to solve any mystery," he said. " He is a gentleman in education and manners. You may trust him, and thoroughly. When it comes to the matter of recompense, refer him to me."

Colonel Deverill did not go back to Devonshire

next day as he had promised.   He was absent from Myrtle Cottage for nearly a week, and when he returned he was accompanied by a gentleman whom he introduced to Mrs. Baddeley as his old friend Melnotte, the famous African traveller.

Leonora was not learned upon the subject of Africa or the Royal Geographical Society.   She had heard such names as Cameron and Stanley, which she associated vaguely with sand, camels, black men, and yellow fever.   She had no love for the Dark Continent.   It gave her neither silk gowns nor high-art furniture; and she was proud to remember that her diamonds were Brazilians. She yawned when her father expatiated upon the interesting experiences of his guest, and put him forward as a man whom it was an honour to know.

"He seems an inoffensive little person," said Leo, "and Tory evidently likes him.   But I cannot imagine him getting the better of a lion, or discovering the source of a river.   And then he is so dreadfully lame!   How did he ever get about Africa with that lame leg?"

" He was not always lame.   His gun burst one day when he was shooting antelopes, and wounded him in the hip."

" Well, he is a rather nice little soul, and I hope he will put you in better spirits," answered Leo lightly.

Her father told her nothing about his interview with St. Austell.   He was unusally grave and silent after his return from London, but on the arrival of an invitation to dinner from Lady Belfield, he hastened to accept it.

" My friend, Melnotte, the African traveller, is staying with me," he wrote, " and I should much like to be allowed to include him in our party."

The messenger who carried Colonel Deverill's note brought back Lady Belfield's reply.

" I shall be charmed to make Mr. Melnotte's acquaintance," she wrote, " though I confess to a lamentable ignorance about Africa. I am prepared to be interested, but not intelligent."

Leonora Baddeley had described Mr. Melnotte accurately when she spoke of him as an inoffensive little person. He was small, with a small round head, close cropped hair, and rather insignificant features. But his eyes were remarkable— luminous, keen, quick, and yet steadfast. Those rather prominent blue-grey eyes had a kindly look too, keen as they were. Mr. Melnotte was not handsome; but he was a pleasant-looking little man, and seemed thoroughly at his ease in a dress coat, in spite of Africa.

"I almost expected to see you with a circle of ostrich feathers standing straight up from your head," said Leonora, laughing, as she stood ready for her fur cloak, gorgeous in black and gold, one of those gowns which defy description and leave only a vague impression of Brussels lace, brocaded velvet, and bullion.

"I left my feathers in Basuto Land," answered Melnotte, "but I sometimes regret a continent upon which I was not obliged to dress for dinner."

He seemed to enjoy himself at the Abbey, whatever his prejudice against civilization. He was graciously received by Lady Belfield; and Sir Adrian talked to him for a great part of the evening, and questioned him closely about his African experiences.

"I have read most of the books upon Africa," said Adrian, "but I blush to say I have not read yours."

"I have not written a book. I have been content to jog along in a very quiet way. I am pretty well-known in a certain part of Africa, but I doubt if anybody has ever heard of me or my adventures. I am not a Fellow of the Geographical."

Sir Adrian knew this beforehand, as he had looked up the list of Fellows and had been surprised at not discovering Melnotte's name.

The traveller's conversation was not the less agreeable because his fame had been somewhat exaggerated by Colonel Deverill. He told a good many interesting anecdotes, some of which were rather familiar to Sir Adrian's ear; but then there must needs be a resemblance between all adventures in a primitive world, where the changes have to be rung upon blacks, buffaloes, lions, alligators, and fever.

Mr. Rockstone, Mr. and Mrs. Freemantle, and their daughter Lucy were of the party, and every one at the table, except Valentine, seemed interested in the lion and buffalo stories, the serious aspect of desert life being relieved by recollections of a comic American, who had been Mr. Melnotte's fellow-traveller at one period. Mr. Belfield heard these anecdotes with a gloomy brow, and was not particularly civil to the narrator.

It was the first time that Valentine had seen his father-in-law since the Colonel's journey to London; and when they were in the billiard-room after dinner, Colonel Deverill took occasion to mention St. Austell's return. Mr. Freemantle and Mr. Melnotte were playing billiards, while Valentine and the Colonel sat on a raised settee at the end of the room, in a panelled recess decorated with breech-loaders of the latest fashion, and rapiers that had been carried by bucks and bloods in the days of Addison and Chesterfield.

Mr. Melnotte played a neat game, but he was a very slow player—aggravatingly slow, Mr. Freemantle thought, when he had to wait through a longish break, his opponent deliberating before every shot, and looking down his cue meditatively before he took his aim.

"A man who can play as well as he does needn't be so confoundedly slow," thought Mr. Freemantle.

Colonel Deverill smoked half his cigar in silence, while Valentine sat by his side, apparently engrossed by watching the game.

"Have you known your African friend long?" he asked presently.

"A longish time."

"He was never at Morcomb, was he?"

"No; he was in Basuto Land when I had Morcomb."

"Ah, to be sure. He is not very yellow, considering he has been so long under an African sun."

"Oh, he has been back over a twelvemonth, knocking about in Ireland," answered the Colonel. "But never mind him. I've got something more important to talk about. I have seen St. Austell."

Valentine's brow darkened, and his colour slowly faded, till even his lips were white.

"When—where?" was all he asked.

The Colonel described the meeting at the Badminton.

"There has been a mistake," he said, in conclusion. "I no longer ask you to divorce your wife. I ask you now to find her. It is your duty to do that, and without an hour's loss of time."

"That is all mighty fine," exclaimed Valentine savagely. "My wife chooses to run away and hide herself, after penning a deliberate avowal of her love for another man—and you tell me it is my duty to find her. I tell you that from the hour she wrote that letter, she was dead to me. It was our final, irrevocable parting. Living or dead she was my wife no longer. You are her father; she has not outraged you—she has not cast you off with scornful words, as she did me. It is for you to look after her."

"You may be sure, Mr. Belfield, that I shall not fail to do a father's duty," answered the Colonel, throwing down the end of his cigar, and grinding it under his heel, to the detriment of the polished parquet.

He felt that Valentine had some justification for repudiating all obligation towards a wife who had written such a letter as that in which Helen had declared her intended flight. That her courage had failed, or that her conscience had been awakened at the last moment, would hardly make atonement to an insulted husband.

CHAPTER VII.

A DECIDED CASE OF DRY-ROT

AFTER that brief conversation with Colonel Deverill in the billiard-room, Valentine Belfield withdrew himself still more from the society of his
fellow-men. Even his appearances in the hunting-
field became spasmodic. He was rarely seen at the
meet, but would contrive to fall in with the hounds
about the middle of the day, and would ride till
the finish like a modern Zamiel, or any other
demoniac character, with a reckless disregard of
his own bones which was only a little less offensive
than his carelessness about other people.

"I believe Belfield must offer a premium for
kicking horses, or he could never get such brutes
as he rides," said Mr. Freemantle, who rode a sober
well-mannered weight carrier, in a sober and
gentleman-like way.

There was a general feeling that Mr. Belfield

had gone altogether to the bad since his wife's disappearance. People pitied him, but wanted to see as little of him as possible. He had never been a favourite in the neighbourhood, and of late his sullen manner had been calculated to alienate even friendship.

And now it had become known that St. Austell was in London, and people—especially the feminine portion of the community—began to be exercised in mind as to what could have become of Mrs. Belfield. Had she eloped with St. Austell, and had they quarrelled and parted after brief union? Or had she never gone off with him? That was the question debated with hushed breath over many an afternoon tea-table.

"Has she any old aunt in Ireland with whom she would be likely to be living?" asked one of the Miss Treduceys. "Most girls have an old aunt that they can go to on an emergency."

"I don't believe Mrs. Belfield has anything so respectable as an old aunt belonging to her," replied Dorothy Toffstaff, who was soured by three unsuccessful seasons in London, during which all the attentions she had received had been too obviously inspired by her father's wealth rather than by her own charms. " My idea is that she went off with St. Austell, as everybody thought at the time of her disappearance, and that he has grown sick of an empty-headed beauty, and has left her in India. She would be sure to get picked up by somebody," added Miss Toffstaff, placidly consigning Mrs. Belfield to the Oriental gutter.

Thus lightly did society at Chadford discuss the problem of a fallen sister's fate; but it was not so lightly that Lady Belfield considered the mystery of her daughter-in-law's disappearance. In a conversation with Colonel Deverill, she drew from him much that had passed between him and St. Austell, and the idea that Helen had changed her mind at the last, after writing that terrible letter, filled her with a new hope.

What more likely than that the erring girl had turned to some conventual sanctuary as the possible shelter from temptation, as Louise de la Vallière in the dawn of love fled from her royal lover to the convent. There only could she find a safeguard against her own passionate heart, an aid for her own weak will. Such a course would account for the unclaimed trunks in the bed-chamber. For the handmaid of heaven, vowed to holy poverty, fine clothes and feminine luxuries were a dead letter.

Impressed with this idea, Lady Belfield resolved to travel quietly through the West of England, visiting all those institutions, Anglican or Roman, to which Helen might possibly have attached herself. She had taken Mr. Rockstone into her confidence, and with his aid she had obtained all the information necessary to guide her search.

She told Adrian nothing of her purpose until her plan was made, and she was on the eve of setting out with her old servant for her companion. The journey would not be a long one. The furthest point was to be the Convent in Lanherne Valley, on the north coast of Cornwall.

To her disappointment, Adrian strongly opposed her scheme.

" Dear mother, no good would result from all

that fatigue and anxiety on your part," he said gently. "I am sure that Helen is not in any such retreat."

"But how can you be sure?"

"Mother, I have reason to know. You must ask me no more. You must have some pity upon me," said Adrian, deadly pale.

"You know that lost girl's fate, and yet hide the truth from me."

"There are secrets that must be kept, that are sacred. Mother, you know how fondly I love you. In my own life there has never been a secret; but in this case I cannot tell you all I know without betraying another person. You would not have me guilty of dishonour."

"No, no; you know I would not. But let me understand—give me some kind of comfort. You know where she is, then—you have known all along?"

Adrian bent his head in assent.

"And yet you have allowed me to torture myself about her?"

"I was tongue-tied."

"I see. She confided in you. It was to her you bound yourself to silence?"

"I can answer no questions."

"But you can tell me that she is safe—happy?"

"She is safe. She did not elope with St. Austell. Her last sin against her husband was the writing of that fatal letter."

"Thank God! But why may I not know her retreat? Why may I not see her again? You know that I loved her as a daughter. Even if she can never be reunited to her husband, she may at least be restored in some measure to me. And there is her poor father, too. Why should he be tortured by uncertainty, or allowed to think that his daughter is leading a wicked life? It is your duty to reveal the truth, Adrian."

"It is my duty to keep my oath. Mother, if you say one word more, I shall regret having trusted you. I beseech you to keep faith with me. Not one syllable to any one, least of all to Valentine."

"Poor Valentine. Can you see him so miserable, and yet not tell him?"

"Nothing I could tell would help him. Mother, the best thing you can do for your own peace of mind—and for us all—is to forget the past so far as it can be forgotten. There is nothing that can be done; nothing. I think you know that I am not without conscience—that I have some sense of duty. If there were anything that could be done I would do it; but there is nothing. As I hope for the life eternal, there is no act of yours or mine that can be of any service to her whose loss we both deplore."

His words and looks were so deeply earnest that his mother could not disbelieve. Adrian had been her strong rock in the last few years; her friend and companion, the one being whose presence always brought brightness and comfort, upon whose sound sense and unselfish affection she could rely. She was mystified, but she was submissive; and the journey to Lanherne was given up.

She told Mr. Rockstone only that she had changed her mind.

"I think you have done right in abandoning

your idea," he said. "Be sure that if Mrs. Belfield is in any retreat of that kind, she will communicate with you before long. Her heart will yearn for you as time goes by, and the longing to see you or to hear from you will be too strong to be repressed by any ascetic rule, however severe."

After that conversation with his mother, Adrian had an uneasy feeling that he had said too much, that he had gone too near the betrayal of his brother's dreadful secret. Yet to have allowed his mother to follow a phantom, to wear out her heart in false hopes and disappointing researches, was more than his duty as a son would allow. His first thought had been of his mother; it was for her sake that he had kept Valentine's secret, and it was for her sake that he had lifted a corner of the veil. It was for her sake that he tried to seem happy when his heart was gnawed by care, and his life darkened by the shadow of fear.

"Let us forget," he had said to her; and often in the long slow days, he had said to himself, "Oh God, if I could but forget!"

His daily walk was by the river. He seemed drawn there by an irresistible attraction. Scarcely a day passed on which he did not stand beside that silent pool, beneath whose dark water lay the murdered wife. He went there oftenest in the twilight, when all things had a vague and ghostly aspect, or when the eye created its own spectres out of the commonest forms. He wondered sometimes that her spirit had never appeared to him, when his thoughts were so full of her. He gazed with melancholy eyes among the shadows of the willow trunks, half expecting to see a spectral form waving tremulously above the bank, like a ghostly Undine. But there was nothing. The dead made no sign.

One evening he saw a red spark shining brightly amidst the grey. It came nearer as he advanced along the path, and presently he found himself face to face with Mr. Melnotte, who was strolling quietly along, smoking a big cigar.

"Good evening, Sir Adrian. A mild night, and a picturesque spot."

"Very. But I should think it must seem uncommonly tame to you after the Zambesi Falls."

"Oh, but I am catholic in my tastes. I can admire an English landscape as heartily as if I had never seen Africa. A favourite walk of yours, Sir Adrian."

"Yes; it is one of my favourite walks."

"I thought so. I have seen you here nearly every evening for the last ten days. I generally take my afternoon stroll in this direction, but on the opposite bank. Lady Belfield was so good as to say I might make free with the park and meadows."

"Naturally. Any friend of Colonel Deverill's would be welcome. Is this your first experience of Devonshire ? "

"Of this side of the county, yes. I know the south coast pretty well. A delightful county."

"You are not a Devonshire man ? "

"I have not that privilege."

There was a silence. Mr. Melnotte did not volunteer any information as to his birth or parentage.   He was a curious little man in this wise, and, except for his African experiences, seemed to be a man without a history.   Sir Adrian wondered how his friendship with Colonel Deverill could have come about.   The two men seemed to have so little in common.   From a good-natured impulse, rather than for any particular reason, he asked Mr. Melnotte to dinner, an invitation which was promptly accepted.

"It is always a pleasure to visit such a house as yours, Sir Adrian," he said.   "A house with a history.   No doubt the Abbey has its history."

"Yes.   It has a good many histories, or traditions."

"Any ghosts?   Any story of a dark crime in the remote past?"

"I have heard of neither ghost nor crime."

"Well, it is a noble old house, even without those embellishments," said Melnotte cheerfully, "and the park and gardens are perfect.   This is a tributary of the Chad, I suppose, this river in your grounds."

"Yes, it unites with the Chad lower down."

" A swift, deepish river, eh ? "

" Swift and deep."

" It makes a very pretty feature in your grounds. Nothing like water for giving beauty and variety to a landscape. To-morrow evening at eight, I think you said, Sir Adrian ? Good night."

Mr. Melnotte crossed a rustic bridge and disappeared in the twilight on the further bank, while Adrian strolled slowly along the cypress walk.

He was met by Lucy Freemantle, who unconsciously suggested a reminiscence of Shakespeare's Beatrice.

" I have been sent to ask you to come to tea," she said, blushing a little, her complexion of lilies and roses looking brighter than ever in the grey winter atmosphere.

" You were very good to take so much trouble about me," answered Adrian, as they shook hands.

" Oh, it was no trouble. I am always glad of a run. Mother and I came to call upon Lady Belfield, and Lady Belfield was getting fidgety about you, so mother told me to run and look for you, and I guessed I should find you this way."

"How clever of you."

They were on very friendly terms, Lucy having known the Abbey and the Abbey people all her life. A few years ago when she had been in the nursery she had looked up to Sir Adrian as a very grand personage, standing as it were apart from all other young men upon the strength of a superior position and superior attainments, but of late she had felt herself more upon a level with him, and more at her ease in his society. He called her Lucy, as a matter of course, having known her in pinafores, but she called him Sir Adrian.

"Is my brother at home?" he asked, as they walked towards the Abbey.

"No, there is no one but Lady Belfield and mother. They are talking parish talk—about the poor old people and their ailments—such dreadful complications. How hard it seems that the poor should suffer in all ways. People who know nothing about them think they are healthy and hardy because of their scanty fare and open air life: but when one comes to know them, one finds that theory a hollow mockery. The open air may be very good for us, but the poor get too much of it."

She spoke warmly, having just come from a scene of suffering in one of the cottages. She was a frank, warm-hearted, energetic girl, tall and strong, in the full bloom of youth and beauty, a girl for whom life meant action and duty, not dress and pleasure. Yet at a county ball she danced as gaily as the most feather-headed of her sisters, and never complained, as they did, of an evening being "slow."

Lady Belfield and Mrs. Freemantle were sitting by the fire in the inner drawing-room, the cosy tea-table and hissing kettle between them. They had been joined by Mr. Rockstone, who sat in one of the most luxurious of the large arm-chairs, with his legs stretched out in front of the hearth, basking in the glow of a friendly fireside, after a long day among his poorest parishioners.

They were talking of Valentine.

"He ought to make an effort, my dear Lady Belfield," said the Vicar. "The blow that has fallen upon him is a heavy one, but it is almost unmanly to succumb as he has done. His whole being is undergoing deterioration. He has brooded upon the one great wrong until his soul has become steeped in gall. He is a misanthrope at an age when men generally love their fellow-creatures. Something must be done to save him from himself."

"Yes, something must be done," echoed Mrs. Freemantle. "It is terrible to see a fine young man like Valentine lapsing into physical and moral decay. My husband tells me that he shuns all his old friends—does not even show at the meet, and rides in a way that proves he cares no more for other people's lives than he does for his own. He ought to go to Australia."

"That is the remedy, Mrs. Freemantle," said the Vicar, "a new country—Australia, or the Red River district—a new and not too civilized country —unfamiliar surroundings. That kind of thing is the only remedy for a mind diseased. I know it would grieve you to part with him, my dear Lady Belfield, but you would have him back in two or three years a new man. Whereas, if you let him stay here, decay is inevitable. You remember what Dickens says about the dry-rot in a man. I'm afraid poor Valentine's is a case of dry-rot."

"I would do anything for his welfare—sacrifice anything," replied Lady Belfield.

"Then you and Adrian must put your heads together and persuade him to travel—California, Texas, Red River, or even Africa, if he fancies shooting antelopes or dealing in buffaloes. You can take advantage of this Mr. Melnotte, who, I am told, is a mighty traveller. The grand thing is to rouse Valentine from his present apathy, and set him going in some way."

"I am entirely of your opinion, Vicar," said Adrian. "My brother wants new surroundings. A young man without aims or interests, moping in a country place, is a sorry spectacle. I will take him in hand to-night."

"Do, my dear Adrian," exclaimed Mrs. Freemantle. "I have known you and your brother too long to be able to see either of you going wrong without speaking my mind."

They sat round the fire for some time after this, talking of many things, enjoying the blaze of the great pine logs and the aroma of Lady Belfield's Indian tea; but two among them were heavy at heart, cheerful as the general tone of the conversation might be. For Adrian there had been no such thing as peace of mind since that fatal night. His life had been one long pretence.

It was a hunting day, and on such days Valentine always stayed out among the latest, rarely appearing until after dinner. He would come into the house on the stroke of eight, perhaps, and would be changing his clothes while the others were dining. He would dine alone between nine and ten, at a little table in front of the billiard-room fire. He had never been a gourmand, but he ate now with the air of a man who hardly knows what he is eating—taking anything the servants set before him, and drinking more than was good for him.

"He ain't got no appreciation of a nice little dinner," said Andrew despondently. "It don't pay to take pains about it, Mrs. Marrable, as I tells cook. Give him a bottle of burgundy and the liqueur stand after dinner, and he asks no questions."

There were no more of those cheery tea-drinkings with the mother after the day's sport; no more recitals of the day's adventures. The young man went out alone in the morning, moody and silent; he came home in the same temper. His mother had watched him in quiet grief, hoping that as the months went by the bruised spirit would recover; but time seemed only to deepen that abiding gloom, and of late she had grown hopeless. Thus it was that she was ready to receive any plausible suggestion for his welfare.

He was late on this particular evening; and it was not until half-past nine that he was ready for his dinner.

"I'll go and talk to him after he has dined," said Adrian, who had been lingering over dessert with his mother, trying to cheer her with the promise of brighter days.

"Do, dear. For pity's sake, influence him for good. I am helpless. His mind is a sealed book to me. He has never confided in me from the time of his boyhood. He has taken his own way always, for good or for evil."

Valentine was sitting in a Glastonbury chair in front of the wide fire-place, the burgundy decanter before him, almost empty. The lamps over the billiard-table were unlighted, and the spacious room was half in shadow. The firelight flickered on guns and swords in the recess at the further end, and there was a circle of soft light round the spot where Valentine sat, from the shaded colza lamp on the small round table.

"A good run, Val?" asked Adrian, seated himself opposite his brother.

" Pretty good."

" You must have killed uncommonly late."

" We killed at sunset, on Plimpsted Ridge."

"But that means five o'clock, and a three-quarters of an hour's ride home. Where have you been since?"

"I don't know."

"Valentine!"

"Don't stare at me, man! I tell you I don't know. I have been riding about somewhere—losing myself on the moor, if you like. Great God, if I could only lose myself altogether—ride away into some enchanted valley, and fall asleep there for ever."

It was almost the first time he had spoken openly of his despair. From the hour of the crime until now there had been no confidence between the brothers. They had lived together, had talked of the daily business of life; but there had been an impassable gulf betwixt the past and the present. By mutual consent they had been dumb.

But to-night Valentine was utterly worn out in mind and body, fagged, helpless, nervous. That powerful frame and strong self-reliant temper had been broken by the slow agonies of remorse. Brutal as the man's nature might be, conscience was not dead in him. It had awakened in the hour when he found himself alone after his crime —face to face with the memory of a murder.

It had never slept since.

"Valentine," began Adrian earnestly, "you are

leading a miserable life. Things cannot go on like this."

" You mean that I had better do as your criminal of the lower classes sometimes does under such circumstances—give myself up—walk into Freemantle's study to-morrow morning and tell him that I killed my wife. Is that what you mean ?"

"No. It is too late for that course. What I mean is that you must leave the scene of your—misadventure. You have lingered here too long. You must go away—to another continent—Africa, Australia, wherever you can find the resources which will give you most relief of mind. The past is past, Val. There is no help for that. Let it be past. You have suffered for your sin of a moment in all the long months that have gone by since that fatal night. You will suffer more or less to the end."

" More or less, no doubt. I have the privilege of an excellent memory," answered Valentine, staring gloomily at the fire.

" Your self-torture can do no good to you or to

any one else. Far away, in the wild free life which suits your temperament, you will at least suffer less. Anything would be better than the stagnation of your existence here."

"You are right. Anything would be better—but I think the best would be death."

"Don't say that, Val. Men have outlived worse sorrows than yours."

"Men are made of very hard wood, and I flattered myself—till last summer—that I was teak or iron-wood: but the dry-rot of remorse has got into me, all the same. I am worm-eaten to the core. Yes, I think you are right, Adrian. I must get away from this place, if I don't want to become a howling lunatic. I have stayed here in a kind of gloomy despair, thinking that I could hardly be more miserable here than anywhere else—but you are right. I have stayed too long. I will stay no longer. Here I am a cause of misery to others as well as to myself. In the desert—or the bush—I shall be my own man again. There will be no need for hypocrisy."

"Your mind will clear and lighten face to face

with unsophisticated nature, Val," said Adrian affectionately. "You will begin a new life. Even the memory of your sorrow will be softened in that far off atmosphere. You will look back upon your old self gently, as we remember the dead. You will have opportunities of helping others—of doing brave and generous deeds. You will be born again, a better and a wiser man. My brother—my beloved brother, the second half of myself, I have infinite faith in you yet." He laid his hand caressingly upon his brother's shoulder. He felt as if a great burden was lifted off his heart by this conversation of to-night. For the first time since the catastrophe that had wrecked both their lives the brothers had spoken together freely. It was like a renewal of brotherly love.

"My dear Adrian, you are a great deal too good to me," said Valentine, and this from him was much.

"You must go away, Val; but you must do nothing hurriedly. Mrs. Freemantle was talking about you to my mother this afternoon, saying that you looked ill and mopish, and needed change.

My mother admitted the fact, and it was agreed that you should be persuaded to travel. Your departure will therefore seem perfectly natural to all this little world of Chadford. There will be no appearance of flight. All you have to think of, therefore, is the place to which you would like to go—all you have to do is to follow the bent of your own inclination."

" I will go to Africa. There is better sport there than in Australia—and a freer life."

" If you decide upon Africa, Melnotte may be of use to you."

" I don't like Melnotte, and I don't believe in his African experiences. I strongly suspect that the man is an impostor. He is too glib."

" But his stories of adventure have a vivid air, as if he had lived among the scenes and people he describes."

" The fellow is a good actor, that is all. Some rowdy adventurer whom the Colonel has picked up in a gambling den. Melnotte may have been to the Cape, perhaps. His experiences in the interior I rank as fiction."

This idea agreed curiously with Adrian's own suspicions as to Mr. Melnotte's truthfulness. Those African stories of his were rather too good and too picturesque to have happened to one traveller. The average man's experiences are dull enough. They ring the changes upon famine, fever, and sport. But Melnotte seemed to have passed from hairbreadth escape to romantic situation, from dramatic encounter to picturesque rescue, with an electrical brilliancy. He had slain his lions by the horde, and shot his gemsbocks in hecatombs. There was exaggeration, no doubt; but whether the man were an actual impostor remained to be proved.

"I don't want anybody's advice?" said Valentine decisively. "If I can once brace myself up to leave this place, I shall go to London, get the kind of outfit I think necessary, and then sail for the Cape. Once there I can pick up all the information I want about the interior, and I shall plan my route from there.

"When will you start?"

"I shall go to London by an early train to-

morrow, and to the Cape by the first good steamer
that can carry me there."

" To-morrow ? That's soon."

" Why should I delay ? I have been staying
here face to face with a spectre—like a man
oppressed by nightmare, who faces some great
horror and cannot move hand or foot. The sooner
I go the better."

" Let me go to London with you, Val. I should
like to see you off."

" No, no. I am not fit company for my fellow-
men yet awhile. Perhaps after ten years in Africa
I may be better. Let me suffer my purgation,
Adrian. Let me wrestle with the memory of sin,
as Jacob wrestled with the angel—and then perhaps
some day "—with a stifled sob—" I shall be better
worthy of your unselfish love—and of my mother."

" God help you to forgetfulness, Val. But let
me go to London with you."

" No, I want to be alone there. I have something to do. I will wire to you before I sail ; and
then, if there were time, and you would like to
come and shake hands at parting———"

"Be sure I will go to you, if you give me the chance. It will comfort the mother to hear of you at the last moment of leaving. She would like to be there herself, dear soul, if you would let her."

"Dear soul, poor soul," murmured Valentine, with a remorseful tenderness which was strange to his rough nature. "She has given me honey, and I have given her gall. I have been a fountain of bitterness to you both. But it is past. Good-night, and good-bye, till I sail. I shall be off early to-morrow morning."

"But you will bid your mother good-bye."

"Must I? That will be hard. I should like to slip away without any leave-taking. I would write to her from London."

"She would be heart-broken if you left her like that."

"Perhaps you are right. It is the weakness of her character to be fond of me. I'll see her in the morning before I start. She will be happier when I am gone—safe and happy—with you. You ought to marry, Adrian. You owe as much to my mother as well as to yourself. There is

Lucy Freemantle, who has been in love with you for the last five years."

" Valentine ! "

" It's a true bill. I've seen the growing passion from the time she left off short frocks and long hair. You have been her idol from the day she left the nursery—perhaps before. I dare say she was often thinking of you over Pinnock or Lingard. Marry her, Adrian. She has not one of the attributes of the typical girl, and will make you a true and honest wife."

" I will wait till my time comes, Val," answered Adrian, with a sad smile. "It has not come yet."

Lady Belfield was always an early riser. She was in her garden next morning, looking at the first daffodils, when Valentine joined her, clad for a journey, in fur-lined overcoat and deer-stalker cap.

" Mother," he began abruptly, " Adrian and I had a long brotherly talk last night, and he advised me to try change of scene as a cure for bitter memories. I am going abroad for a spell."

"Yes, dear.　Yes, it will be a good thing, I am sure," answered his mother, paling suddenly at the mere thought of a possible parting; "but you will not be going just yet.　You will take time to think about it."

"I am going at once.　You know I was never given to irresolution.　I have done most things, for good or evil, on the spur of the moment.　I am off by the 8.35.　My portmanteaux have gone down to the stable yard.　I shall stay a day or two in town, and then sail for the Cape."

"For the Cape!　That is so far, Val.　Why not go to Italy or Spain."

"Tame, hackneyed, intolerable.　The holiday ground of self-opinionated Yankees and personally conducted Cockneys.　No, if change of scene is to do me any good, if I am to get out of myself, I must get face to face with Nature.　Africa is the place for me.　Don't be afraid, dear mother.　The Dark Continent is as safe a solitude as Herne Bay."

"And you are going—this morning?"

"At once.　The dog-cart is waiting for me. Good-bye."

He clasped his mother in his arms, kissed her as he had not kissed her for years—hardly since he was a schoolboy. His own eyes were not innocent of tears as he rushed away, leaving her to sob out her sorrow in the secluded shrubbery walk which her footsteps had so often trodden. Never had she felt more desolate than in this parting with her wayward son, and yet she told herself that it was well he were gone. Anything must be better than to see him as he had been since last August.

The South-Western Railway conveyed Mr. Belfield to Exeter, but at the junction there he had a choice of lines, and the Great Western suited him best on this occasion. He crossed from one platform to the other, took his ticket for Paddington, and came out upon the departure platform of the Great Western, under the big clock.

The platform was not so crowded as usual, and the train was not due for five minutes. As he walked slowly towards the end of the station, Valentine passed a man whose face flashed upon him like the sight of a ghost in high noon.

The wintry sun shone upon those pale and high-bred features. He saw the face looking at him, half in hatred, half in scorn, and he could not give back scorn for scorn, hate for hate. He who had never feared his fellow-men sickened at the sight of this man, and passed on with quickened step, and eyes looking steadily forward, pretending not to see that familiar face, the face of the man who had stolen his wife's heart.

St. Austell stopped and looked back at him.

"As I am alive, that was the face of a felon," he said to himself; " and the mystery of Helen's fate is darker that any of us imagine. That man dared not meet my eye, although it was his place to hector and mine to quail. There was guilt in that look."

He was on his way westward. Since that meeting at the Badminton he had been much disturbed in his mind about his lost love. Fickle as the previous experience of his life had proved him, he had not yet forgotten Helen. The year which Mrs. Baddeley had allowed for the duration of his passion was not yet ended, and it may be that the disappointment and mischance which had attended this particular intrigue had intensified his feelings. He would have forfeited ten years of his life to have found Helen and won her for his own : but there was that in her husband's countenance which chilled his soul. He had half a mind to follow Valentine Belfield, and tax him then and there with foul play. He had no evidence except the mystery of the wife's disappearance and that guilty look in the husband's face, but the two together brought conviction to St. Austell's mind.

CHAPTER VIII.

VALENTINE BELFIELD walked to the furthest end of
the platform and stood there, cold and sick, like a
man in an ague fit, till his train came in from
Plymouth, and then he had to run after the train
as it steamed into the station, and scramble into a
first-class compartment, panting and breathless, and
white to the lips.

"You oughtn't to run things so close as that,
sir. You don't look the kind of man who can
stand it," said an elderly parson, one of those
amiable busybodies who are always interested in
other people's affairs.

Valentine scowled at him by way of answer,
as he threw his deer-stalker into the rack, and
mopped his forehead and hair, damp with icy
sweat.

"A churlish personage," thought the parson;

"something wrong with the heart, and a very irritable temper;" and the good man tried to interest himself in his newspaper, glancing over the top of it every now and then to see if there were any hope of conversation.

Valentine put on his cap again, pulled it over his forehead, and coiled himself in the corner of the carriage in an attitude that meant total isolation. He was trying to recover his nerve after that sudden apparition of St. Austell.

"By ——, I was afraid of the man," he said to himself. "For the first time in my life I have known what it is to fear the face of a man. If a brace of constables came to arrest me, warrant and handcuffs complete, I wouldn't flinch; but his face unnerved me. He loved her. He would ask me, 'What have you done with your wife? What have you done with that frail, false girl, whose heart was mine?' Yes, his, *his*—not mine. It was *his* love I murdered. It is to *him* I am answerable. It was *his* life I spoiled. She had ceased to belong to me—she was openly, avowedly his. And I quailed before him, turned sick with fear at sight of the villain who wrouged me."

For an hour and more he sat in his corner, living over that brief meeting on the platform, seeing that passing vision of a malignant face, telling himself again and again, in bitterest mockery, that it was St. Austell who had lost by that fatal blow. At last, and with a tremendous effort, he dismissed this dark train of thoughts, and his mind recurred to one of the objects of his journey to London.

Ever since his last meeting with Madge Darley, the girl and her mission had been present to his mind. Passion was dead in him, buried under the crushing weight of a great remorse, numbed and frozen as the senses are in a nightmare. There was no rekindling of an old flame; but in the ashes of his dead love for that strange girl there was a faint glow, a little spot of warmth, where all else had grown cold. He yearned for her presence, for the sound of her voice, for the touch of her hand. He felt that if there could be comfort or hope for him anywhere upon this earth it would be with her. He felt that if there were any one to whom he could confess his crime, it was Madge Darley, and not a priest.

"The Forlorn Hope," he repeated to himself as he sat in his corner, looking out at the landscape: every field, and copse, and hill, and curving stream familiar to him from his boyhood; beheld again and again at all seasons, sometimes in listless vacuity, sometimes in feverish impatience.

At last the train steamed into Paddington Station on the edge of dusk. The sunset glowed red athwart the London fog as the train passed Harrow and Hanwell. The great vaulted roof of the terminus looked sepulchral in the chilly light of electric lamps.

Valentine told a porter to take his portmanteaux to the Great Western Hotel, and then left the station on foot. He was going to Lisson Grove to look for the Refuge founded by Madge Darley.

The long thoroughfare of the Grove was light with gas-lit shops, and full of traffic. Valentine inquired in one of the shops, and was directed to a side street—a dismal looking street of shabby, dilapidated houses, which might have had pretensions to respectability half a century ago, but which had fallen to about the lowest stage in the history of bricks and mortar. They were twelve-roomed houses, however, and afforded accommodation to a considerable population, as appeared by the various lighted windows, suggestive of several domiciles under one roof.

Across the front of one of these houses, of a somewhat better aspect than its neighbours, appeared a long black board on which the words, "The Forlorn Hope," were painted in large white letters. In front of the fanlight there was a lamp with the words " Refuge for Homeless Women and Girls," in black letters, on the glass. There was no possible mistake as to the motive and character of this institution.

The door swung open at Valentine's touch, and as he crossed the threshold a woman in a black gown and white cap came out of the parlour next the street, and met him in the passage.

It was Madge Darley. The shepherdess was

always ready to receive the lost sheep. The fold was humble and unattractive, but it meant what it offered—shelter.

She started at sight of a tall man in a fur-bordered coat — started again on recognizing Valentine.

" Mr. Belfield ! " she exclaimed.

" Yes. I told you I should come to you some day, Madge, and you promised not to shut your door in my face."

" I am not likely to do that ; but I don't think you will want to stay very long in this house."

She led the way into the parlour, a plainly fur-nished room, lighted by a cheap paraffin lamp, under a green shade.

A tall press, made of pitch pine, occupied either side of the fire-place. The table was of varnished deal, the walls were whitewashed, the floor was uncarpeted, and half a dozen rush-bottomed chairs completed the furniture of the room ; but all was scrupulously neat and clean. A fire burned cheerily in the shining grate, and an open-work brass fender made one point of brightness in the picture. A large iron kettle was singing on the old-fashioned hob.

"Pray sit down," said Madge, pointing to a chair opposite her own. "You have an idle hour to spare, I suppose, and you have come to see our Refuge—to find out for yourself whether we are doing good work—in order that you may help us."

She spoke gravely, faltering a little, more deeply moved by his presence in that place than she would have cared to own to herself. The lesson of her life for nearly four years had been the lesson of forgetfulness; but it was not yet learned. His presence had still the power to awaken an un-reasoning gladness, to give life a new colour.

"No, Madge; I am no philanthropic philanderer. I confess to caring very little whether your work of mercy thrive or fail. I am here from pure selfish-ness. I am eaten up by my own cares; my own burden is too heavy for me; and of late, night and day, I am devoured by one thought, one hope——"

He stopped suddenly, looking at her with eyes

that shone feverishly bright in his haggard face, with one strong hand clenched upon the table between them.

" The Forlorn Hope, Madge," he said in a low voice, after a few moments' silence, " the hope that you will pity me when no one else in this world, except my brother, can pity me, knowing all. Yes, that you, knowing my sin, might still pity me— might still love me."

He flung himself on his knees at her feet. He seized her hand and covered it with kisses, despairing kisses, which moved her more than his passion of days gone by had ever moved her, fondly as she had loved the tempter.

She snatched her hand from him indignantly, looking at him in angry surprise.

" I thought you knew me better than to talk to me in the old strain," she said. " I thought I had shown you that I am not the kind of woman to be tempted by a fine gentleman lover—to be tempted now, after I have given my life to the saving of weaker women. Do you think that I am likely to forget that you are another woman's husband—and that when you were free you refused to marry me?"

"I was a fool, Madge, a self-opinionated idiot. I did not know that you were the one woman upon this earth who could have made my life happy— who might have influenced me for good. I was bound round by petty prejudices, by bigoted belief in birth and position. What are birth and position when weighed against the nobility of such a nature as yours? I saw in you only a beautiful peasant, whom it was my business, as a gentleman, to seduce. And when I saw that your resistance was real and earnest, I lost my temper, and fancied myself in love with another woman. It was pique that made me Helen Deverill's lover."

He shuddered as he pronounced his wife's name.

"That is all past and done with," said Madge gravely. "I am very sorry that your marriage ended unhappily; but there is a long life before you yet, I hope, and there must be something for you to do in it. And now I must see after my patients. It is tea-time. Shall I make you a cup of tea?"

She went to one of the presses, opened it, and began to take out cups and saucers, and little crockery tea-pots, and trays, and plates. Everything was of the cheapest, but the things had been chosen for their prettiness, and the little trays had a neat and dainty look as those active hands arranged them, each with its spotless linen d'oyley.

"Yes, please. I should relish a cup of cold water from your hand. And my mouth is parched and full of dust after my journey. Think of me as the worst of your patients. Have you many in the house?"

"Every bed is full except one. There is a girl of nineteen in the next room, dying. If you could hear her story you would know what misery means."

She was moving to and fro between the press and the fire-place, filling her little tea-pots from the big copper kettle as she talked to him.

"I need not wait for that. I know the meaning of misery."

"Ah, but not of such misery as she has suffered, a girlhood that has been one long degradation. Think of what it was for that girl to awaken to the first consciousness of life in the midst of such surroundings as decent lips dare not name; to have been so reared as not to know the meaning of sin till she was steeped in it, blackened by it, dying of it. That is her history."

"She is what you call an interesting case, I suppose."

"She is one among many. Old and young come here every day, pleading for a corner to die in. That is about all we can give yet awhile."

"You have done a good deal, I think, in establishing such a refuge."

"People are so kind. The poor have helped me as much as the rich. Those who have had no money to give have brought me little presents out of their household goods, at a sacrifice. This copper kettle was given by a widow who goes out charing. It was a legacy from a butcher's wife whom she had served for years. 'It is too good for me, Sister,' she said.' Any little tin tea kettle will do to make my cup of tea.' She kissed the lid of the kettle before she handed it to me, for love of her dead mistress."

She set one of the tea-trays before him, with a little plate of bread and butter, such as she had been cutting for her patients. She rang a bell, and a woman of about forty came into the room, dressed in a grey merino gown and a white cap and apron. She looked like a lady, but she was very thin and gaunt, with a pale pinched face and a sad smile. She looked surprised at finding a stranger seated by the hearth. "Sister Angela, Mr. Belfield," said Madge, by way of introduction. "Mr. Belfield is good enough to be interested in our work, Sister." Angela bowed, but made no reply. The two women took half a dozen of the little trays between them, and went away to attend to their patients, leaving Valentine to stare into the fire and brood over his past life.

He thought of those careless days on the river, with boat and dog and gun : the sheer idleness of fancy which had led him to Madge Darley's cottage; the hold her beauty had taken of him, and his scornful disbelief in her virtue. And he now came to this woman in his agony, as the one woman who could give him help and comfort, whose strong brave soul could inspire him with courage to begin life anew. And having come into this house of pain, he felt as if it would be best of all to stay here for ever, to be her clerk, her helper, her drudge, only to have the privilege of being near her. He half forgot his scheme of distant travel; he was ready to grovel at her feet and plead to be allowed to stay with her.

She was absent for more than an hour. He emptied the tea-pot, and looked at his watch a dozen times before she came back.

"Are you surprised to see me here still?" he asked.

"Yes, I thought you would have gone back to your hotel. This is not a place for you."

"I suppose not; yet you told me if I were in distress I might come to you for shelter. I hoped to find the name of your house was not altogether a delusion—The Forlorn Hope. I have no other hope, Madge."

"That cannot be true. You have your mother, who adores you."

"My mother cannot help me to bear my burden. It would blast her declining years, bring her in anguish to the grave, to know all my misery. I want some strong bosom to lean upon; I want some heroic soul to inspire me with courage. Madge, I have come to you—to you,.as the only woman who can shed a ray of light upon this darkened spirit. I am a viler sinner than any of your lost sheep. Have pity upon me if you can, Madge, for I am the kind of sinner whom no one pities. I am a murderer."

He clasped her hand in both his own, and drew her nearer to him, looking up at her with despairing eyes, as she stood looking down upon him, speechless with horror.

"I killed my wife."

"Oh, God!"

"I had the confession of her falsehood in my hand, her declaration that she had ceased to love me, and that she was passionately in love with another man—that she was leaving me to be his mistress. A pleasant letter for a husband to read, Madge. The ink was wet upon the paper, and she stood there looking at me—beautiful—false to the core. I struck her to the ground. It was only one blow, but it killed her. Between the reading of that letter and her death there was but an interval of half a dozen seconds. The ink was wet still, and she was lying at my feet looking up at me—dead."

"It was horrible," gasped Madge, "an awful, irreparable calamity—but not murder. You did not mean to kill her."

"I will not say as much as that. I think I wanted to kill her—as I would have killed her seducer had he been there—but I was sorry the instant she was dead. The agony of remorse began before that ink was dry."

"You should have confessed the truth; you should have braved all consequences."

"I should. I was a coward and a fool; a craven, to shrink from the consequences of my wrath. I had a right to be angry. I forgot how frail a thing she was. She fell like a lily—a tall white lily snapped in a storm. One moment—my passion had vented itself—and she was dead."

And then he went on to describe that ghastly burial of the dead, in the silence of the summer night. He dwelt on every detail, showing how vividly every circumstance of that dismal scene had painted itself upon his memory. He recalled these things shudderingly, as a man relates a bad dream which he has dreamed again and again.

" Did no one suspect you ? "

" No one has found me out. There is a man I suspect of being some kind of eavesdropper and spy—a man who is on a visit to her father, and who passes for a gentleman."

" You must not lose an hour in getting away from England—from Europe—beyond the reach of pursuit, if that be possible. Suspicion once aroused, detection might be easy, and then, having hidden your crime, you might seem a deliberate murderer instead of the victim of a moment's passion. You must sail by the first ship that can carry you. Go to Liverpool to-night by the mail

—if Liverpool is the port—and start to-morrow morning."

"I am in no hurry."

"But if your secret were once suspected, to leave England then would look light flight, and only confirm suspicion. Go at once, while you are free to go."

"I have half a mind to stay and take my chance," he answered thoughtfully. "If you would be kind to me, Madge—if you would let me spend an hour in this room sometimes, hear the sound of your voice, watch you coming in and going out, I would rather stay in London than go to Africa to look for diamonds and shoot big game. I am not the man I was before that night, Madge. When—when I had done that deed, my first thought was to save my neck—to hide my crime and go scot-free. I thought life would be the same as it had been—the hunting-field—the race-course—the battue—all the same. I thought I could forget. But when the seasons came round again, and the old sports, and the old people—my God, what a change ! All the zest was gone. I went about as if I was in a dream, only half conscious of my own existence or the life round me. Wherever I went, the same haunting thoughts went with me, and a ghost that would not be laid. Oh, Madge, you are stronger than I— braver, nobler. Pity me if you can, as the strong should pity the weak."

"I do pity you, poor soul, with all my heart," she answered softly.

She bent over him and kissed his burning forehead. For the first time in their lives her lips touched him in love, freely given.

"God bless you, Madge, for that kiss," he faltered. "It shows me that you can pity me. Oh, my love, don't banish me. Let me stay near you —always. Let me serve you as a slave serves his master. Let me wear a suit of fustian and corduroy, and carry coals and clean windows for you —until you have tried me by years of faithful service, if you like. God knows I will be patient in consideration of the wretch I am: and then when you have found that there is some good in me, let me be your husband, and let us go away together to the other end of the world. If there is happiness for me upon this earth, it must be found with you."

She looked at him in silence, with a slow, sad smile, for some moments before she answered.

"That is all a dream, Mr. Belfield, a feverish dream of your poor sick soul. I have my duty here, which I shall never leave; and you have your duty to yourself, and to your mother and brother. Think how their lives would be darkened if you were brought to answer for your crime, and made to appear that which you were not—a deliberate murderer. For their sake you ought to get away while the coast is clear. Begin a new life in a new country. Find new duties, as I found mine when my life was most desolate; and in doing your duty and saving the souls of sinners, you may find atonement for your own sin. And then the shadows will be lifted, the burden will be lessened, the light will come."

"I cannot live without you, Madge. I have yearned for you in my misery. That kiss has sealed me as your own for ever."

"If you persist in saying these things, I will never see you again, Mr. Belfield. I have done with all thoughts of love. I have planned out my path in life, and mean to keep to it. And now I must wish you good-night, and ask you to leave this house. I have a great deal to do before bedtime."

" Cannot other people do it for you? Cannot you give one evening in your life to my despair— you who do so much for others?"

" I am the head of our little organization, and have to see that all is done rightly. There are three-and-twenty sick or ailing girls and women in the house, and only three sisters besides myself to see to them. We are a sisterhood of twenty-two. I am the only permanent resident. The other twenty-one each give one day and night in every week to the work. They come at eight one evening and go away at eight on the following evening. It is one day taken from the week of worldly business for a work of mercy. We find the plan answer better than many resident sister- hoods. The sisters are more cheerful, better tempered, and in better health. Their lives are not monotonous.   There is no weariness, no pining for escape into the outer world. They always bring a certain amount of freshness to their work; and it makes them happy to know that, however worldly the rest of their lives may be, one day out of seven is spent in doing good."

"The plan is your invention, I suppose?"

"Yes, it is mine."

"Clear brain—strong heart! Why did I not know your value four years ago? Well, Madge, you have received me kindly, and I won't impose upon your kindness. Good-night. I shall come again to-morrow evening."

"Think better of it, and go to Liverpool by the night mail."

"Good-night," he repeated, ignoring her injunction.

"Good-night."

They clasped hands and parted. Scarcely had the outer door shut upon him, when she covered her face with her hands and burst into tears.

"Oh, my love, my sin-stained love!" she

murmured; " I care for you more in your abasement than I ever cared for you yet. I would
give my life to lead you back to happiness, if I
had any hope you could ever be happy.   But the
curse of blood is on your soul, and what hope can
there be for you on this side of the grave ? "

CHAPTER IX.

"IT WAS THE BRAND OF CAIN"

MRS. BADDELEY was very tired of the River Chad, and of the rustic garden where the crocuses starred the lawn with their golden cups. It was all very rural and fresh and innocent, but she had an aching void where her heart should have been, and longed for London dissipations as the only anodyne for care. The good kind fellow, whom she had talked of so cheerily last season while he was broiling under an Indian sun, was on his way home now; and she could not think without some uneasiness of the manner in which he would take things when he should arrive, good-natured as he was.

It is not a pleasant thing for a husband to come home and find a sheaf of bills, and lawyers' letters, and County Court summonses awaiting him, or to find his household gods subject to a bill of sale held by a West-end dressmaker; and this was exactly the condition of affairs that awaited Major Baddeley.

He was to leave Bombay in February, and now February and the crocuses were waning, and in all probability the Major had started.

"I shall get a telegram from Aden before I know where I am," said the anxious wife. "I think I ought to go back to London, Dad."

"You can at least stay till you get your telegram."

Mrs. Baddeley sighed, yawned, and resumed her novel. The romances supplied by Mudie were her only resources in this sleepy country life. She, who in London seldom opened a book, devoured three volumes in a day.

"Poor Frank! How I wish somebody would leave him a fortune!" she said, with her eyes on the page. "He would be such a perfect husband if he had only three or four thousand a year. How long is your friend Mr. Melnotte to stay with us?"

"Does he bore you?"

"Not at all. He is very inoffensive, and he plays écarté with you of an evening; but I can't quite understand why you asked him here."

"There is more in him than anybody supposes," replied the Colonel. "I like his conversation, and, if you are going to desert me, I shall keep him as long as I can."

Leo yawned assent. The African traveller had not inspired the faintest interest in her thoroughly feminine breast. Her only idea of sport was a prettily shaped horse that went like the wind, and a perfectly fitting habit. Big game and the hardships of life in the desert did not engage her fancy.

After luncheon she went for a long ramble by the river, not because she loved the river or the landscape, but because she knew that open-air exercise was good for her figure and complexion.

Mr. Melnotte was out and about almost all day. He seemed to be as keenly interested in rustic explorations and village gossip as in the perilous adventures of the desert. He made friends everywhere, talked to every one, and had a pleasant, homely way, which put every one at ease with him. He was out on the day after Valentine's departure, when Sir Adrian called at Colonel Deverill's cottage early in the afternoon.

Adrian was shown into the drawing-room. Mrs. Baddeley was out walking, the butler told him, but the Colonel was at home.

The Colonel was not very prompt to appear, having lately settled himself in his arm-chair by the dining-room fire, to sleep off the effects of a heavy lunch and a pint of dry sherry. Adrian was left to himself for at least ten minutes, during which time he walked up and down the drawing-room restlessly, full of thought.

There was a small writing-table in one of the windows, and a chair in front of it, which looked as if it had been occupied that morning. On the table there was a pile of volumes with the label of the Royal Geographical Society upon all of them, and beside the books there was an inkstand and a blotter.

Sir Adrian had the curiosity to look at these

books.   Cameron, Livingstone, Stanley.   They
were all books of African travel.   He opened one
of the volumes at the places marked with slips of
paper.

At each of the marked places he found an anec-
dote, and every one of those anecdotes had been
recited by Mr. Melnotte at the Abbey dinner-table
or in the Abbey billiard-room as personal adventures.

He opened another volume with the same result,
and then another, in which there were more selected
anecdotes which had not yet been related, stock-in-
trade for future evenings.

" Valentine was right," he said to himself;
" Melnotte is an impostor."

But why was the man there if an impostor?
Colonel Deverill was not a man to be taken in by
any common swindler.   There must be some reason
for the presence of this sham explorer.

Was there some hidden motive in his visit to the
Colonel : some motive which involved danger to
Valentine?

Adrian had been not a little perplexed by Colonel

Deverill's choice of that river-side cottage as a winter residence; and now it seemed to him that Melnotte was a mysterious ally of the Colonel's, who had been brought there to act as a spy upon the inmates of the Abbey.

To suppose this was to suppose that Helen's father suspected the dark secret of his daughter's fate, and such a supposition was full of terror.

Colonel Deverill came into the room while Adrian was still standing by the table, with Cameron's book in his hand. He put it down as he went forward to greet the Colonel.

"Your friend Melnotte seems fond of reading other people's adventures," he said carelessly.

The Colonel glanced from his visitor to the books on the table, and at once accepted the situation.

"Yes, he is never so happy as when he has his nose in a volume of travels," he answered. "You are not looking over well, Adrian. What's the matter?"

"Oh, I am well enough."

"But a little anxious about your brother," pursued the Colonel, watching Sir Adrian's face as he spoke. "I met Mrs. Freemantle in my stroll this morning, and she told me you were all of you uneasy about Mr. Belfield, and that you wanted him to travel."

"Yes; he is out of health and out of spirits."

"Everybody has noticed the change in him. There has been a deeper gloom than husbands usually fall into under such circumstances. Most men take their troubles pretty lightly, nowadays."

Adrian was silent.

"Have you succeeded in persuading your brother to try change of scene?"

"I hope so. There is nothing decided. Valentine is not given to allowing other people to manage his life. He went up to town yesterday to look about him."

"Oh, he has gone to London, has he? Where does he put up?"

"I really don't know. At the Great Western, most likely, if he took the train for Paddington. If he travelled by the other line, he may have gone to the Grand."

" You have not heard from him since he left ? "

" No ; he is not fond of letter writing. He will telegraph if he has anything to communicate."

The conversation drifted to indifferent matters, but was far from lively. Colonel Deverill had a preoccupied air, and looked out of the window oftener than was natural to a well-mannered Irishman.

Adrian was rising to leave when the butler flung open the door and announced " Lord St. Austell."

" By Jove, this is an unexpected pleasure," said the Colonel; and before he could recover from his surprise, Sir Adrian passed St. Austell with the coldest possible salutation, nodded good-bye to his host, and departed.

" What brings you into this part of the world ? " asked Colonel Deverill, when the door had shut upon Adrian.

" I want to know the result of Melnotte's investigations, and I was sick of waiting for letters. He has been very slow."

" Yes ; he has been uncommonly slow. I can

get nothing out of him. And now Belfield has given us the slip. If there has been foul play, he may be on his way to America by this time—safe out of reach before we can move a step. He went up to London yesterday."

"I know he did," answered St. Austell. "I met him in the station at Exeter."

"You did?   Strange."

"Yes, it was a strange meeting, for it confirmed my darkest suspicions. We met face to face, Deverill—met and passed each other ; and if ever I saw the face of a murderer I saw it then."

"Bosh ! Men don't wear the record of crime on their faces."

"This one wore it yesterday : it was the brand of Cain. He quailed at the sight of me, at me—his wife's lover, the man who blighted his married life. Why, if he had not been the greater sinner, he would have blazed up—flown at me like a tiger—tried to strangle me. Was it natural to turn livid and then pass on, pretending not to see me ? Was that the conduct of the man whom I had wronged—who had the right to call me to account ? No, Deverill ; it was the manner of a wretch who knew himself a hundred times more guilty than I. It was the face of an assassin. And you and Melnotte have trifled with your chances, have let this murderer get clear off before you have discovered his crime."

" I do not think Melnotte has been idle ; but I can get very little out of him. He is uncommonly close."

" Yes, that is a trick of the trade. I believe this one is really a clever fellow. He began life as a gentleman, and started in his present profession with the advantage of a university education. He was a man who might have done well in life, perhaps, if it had not been for an intrigue with a Belgian countess, which finished in a duel with her husband. He got a bullet in the hip which lamed him for life. They think highly of him at Scotland Yard, and he has been invaluable to me in two or three rather awkward affairs. But I don't like his letting things hang fire. He has been here long enough to arouse Belfield's suspicions. When do you expect him ? "

"Any time between now and eight o'clock. He always dines with us, and if you can stay to dinner——",

"Of course I can stay. I came to Devonshire to find out what progress you were making. I cannot rest till I know the worst; and if there is a wrong to be avenged I shall never rest till vengeance has been done. I'll take a stroll and a smoke by the river, and then go back to the inn and dress. I shall be with you soon after seven, on the chance of getting some talk with Melnotte before dinner."

He left the Colonel free to resume his easy chair by the dining-room fire, his newspapers, cigar, and afternoon sleep. Colonel Deverill was in the lowest spirits, full of vague dread, as one upon the threshold of a ghastly revelation; but there are phases of physical comfort which can coexist with mental depression, and the Colonel went back to his fireside and his soft, warm chair, his brandy-and-soda and afternoon slumbers, as naturally as the dog goes to the hearthrug and coils himself round by the fender, even after he has been kicked.

St. Austell lighted his cigar and sauntered along by the river, shadowed now by woods that were leafless, and hills that were bleak and bare. A heron came swooping over the tree tops and down to the water's edge, and stood on one leg in a meditative attitude, waiting to spear the first unwary fish that swam near. The sky was grey and dull, but the air was mild. It was an atmosphere suggestive of idleness and languid emotions.

St. Austell followed the course of the Chad as far as the mouth of that tributary stream which flowed through the grounds of Belfield Abbey, but at this point he turned, and went along the narrow woodland path which led to those shrubberied walks where he had last seen Helen Belfield. It was summer then, and the foliage was dense and heavy, shutting out the world beyond that leafy solitude. Now all was bleak and bare, save where the conifers showed darkly green against the dull grey sky. He remembered every turn of the path by which they two had walked, he pleading, she listening, with drooping head and eyelids heavy with tears.

" I know she loved me," he told himself. " If she had lived she would have been mine. Or if she had made up her mind to throw me over, and live her life without me, she would not have left me in uncertainty about her fate, she would not have trifled with my love and tortured me for no purpose. She is dead, and that man has murdered her."

He was close to the spot where they had sat together under the willow upon that last afternoon. Yes, there was the cypress walk, and there below it, upon the edge of the stream, the great grey trunk of the willow slanting across the bank, and there the rustic bench upon which they had sat.

Some one was sitting there to-day—a woman in a fur coat, with just the same graceful, curving line of throat and shoulders, and small head with heavy coils of hair. His heart stood still at sight of that figure. It was she. She had been living at the Abbey all this time in hiding. She was there, almost within reach of his arms. In that one delirious moment he felt that he loved her as he had never loved woman yet, with an undying love.

She rose at the sound of his footsteps and came slowly forward to meet him, a black poodle by her side, shaking the silver bell on his collar as he ran. St. Austell's heart sank as she drew nearer, with the bitterest disappointment he had ever felt in his life.

"Mrs. Baddeley, you have given me a crushing blow," he said slowly. "I took you for your sister."

"Poor Helen. You of all people ought least to expect to find her sitting here."

"You still believe that I was concerned in her disappearance?"

"I have not yet reconciled myself to any other idea."

"Would to God you were right, and that I knew where to find her. I am tortured by the belief that she was made away with by her husband."

And then he told Mrs. Baddeley of that chance encounter at Exeter, and of the conclusions he had drawn from Mr. Belfield's countenance.

" Is not that rather too strong an interpretation to put upon a disagreeable face ? " said Leo dubiously. " Short of clairvoyance I cannot understand your ground for such an idea."

" Call it clairvoyance, if you like—the clairvoyance of love. I know that, as I looked the man in the face, a hideous fancy flashed into my mind. That man is the murderer of my love. I shall never rest till I have solved the mystery of her fate. If she is alive, I will find her. If she is dead, I will find out how she died ; and if there was foul play her murderer shall not go unpunished."

Leonora Baddeley looked at him in silence for some moments, half in cynical disbelief, half in admiration. Had he but loved her with such a love as that, she would have counted the world well lost for his sake. He had sued to her and had been rejected, because she had loved the world's good word better than she loved him, and, perhaps still more, because she doubted the reality of his love. And then afterwards, when she saw his affections transferred to her sister—saw him ever so much more earnest in the pursuit of that newer fancy, she had discovered her own weakness, and that he was the one man whom she really loved. Tortured by jealousy, she found out how dear he had been to her—he whom she had treated so lightly, holding him at bay with careless speeches and silvery laughter, and all the polished arts of a coquette, as she had done with a cloud of meaner admirers. Only of late had she known what it was to love and have her love unreturned.

" You talk very big," she said, " but you have done nothing to solve the mystery."

" Directly, nothing ; but through your father I hope to accomplish everything."

" My poor father. He is very unhappy about Helen."

" He will have to be still more unhappy, if her fate was as dreadful as I think."

" Poor father. It would be too hard upon him in his old age. But I cannot believe in this morbid fancy of yours. The mystery of my sister's disappearance has set us all imagining horrors. She is safe enough, I dare say—hiding herself somewhere, and not caring one little bit for our anxiety."

"If I could only think as much—if I could only hope as much," St. Austell answered gloomily.

They walked back towards the cottage together, talking very little, both of them serious and depressed. Mrs. Baddeley was far from being easy in her mind about her sister, although she affected to make light of St. Austell's fears.

CHAPTER X.

THE SECRET OF THE RIVER

It was ten o'clock, and Mrs. Baddelcy was sitting by the drawing-room fire, with Tory and a novel for her only companions, while Lord St. Austell, Colonel Deverill, and Mr. Melnotte remained in the snug little dining-room. St. Austell and the Colonel sat on each side of the fire, with their faces in shadow. Melnotte was at the table, in the bright light of the moderator lamp, with a note-book in his hand, to which he referred now and again in the course of his narrative or statement.

"You think I have been slow, Lord St. Austell," he said, "and that by my dilatory way of going to work I have lost my man. All I can say is that I don't think I have lost my man, and that this was a case in which precipitate action would have been fatal. I had to be sure of my facts before I took any step in the open.

"The first thing to be done was to find out how, and when, and with whom, Mrs. Belfield left the Abbey on the night on which she was supposed to have run away; or whether she ever left the Abbey at all. A long and careful investigation, involving the cross-examination of every official at the station and every fly-driver in Chadford, convinced me that she did not leave the Abbey on that night, or on the following morning, or on any subsequent occasion. From the hour when she wrote that letter of which Colonel Deverill informed me she was never seen by mortal eye; unless it was by Sir Adrian, or his mother, or Mr. Belfield.

"I have a knack of getting friendly with people upon a very slight pretence, and I contrived to get on friendly terms with Lady Belfield's housekeeper, Mrs. Marrable, an admirable old woman, and as easy to manage as a child; a devoted servant, and loyal to the backbone; but an incorrigible prattler. All she wanted was a pretext for prattling, and I found one for her. I called one afternoon when the family were out, and asked, as if in sheer frivolity, to see the old oak panelling, and the carved banister rails in the gallery over the hall. If Mrs. Marrable would be kind enough to show me the upper floor, I should esteem it a favour, I said; and as I had given the grey-haired footman half-a-crown when I dined at the Abbey, he at once produced Mrs. Marrable.

"From Mrs. Marrable I ascertained that Mr. Belfield was not at the Abbey at the time of his wife's disappearance and had not been there for months; that he did not come there until quite a week after that event, when he arrived late in the evening, and told his mother that he had lost money at York Races and had gone over to Paris for a few days to revive his spirits. Mrs. Marrable was certain that he said he had been in Paris. It was a way with him before he was married to go off to Paris at an hour's warning, and she wondered what attraction there could be in such a place for a young English gentleman.

"Having ascertained from this good soul that Mr. Belfield had *not* been at the Abbey on the night of August the 19th, my next business was to ascertain from other people that he *had* been there on that particular night. I had made myself pretty sure of that fact from the porter who took his ticket at Chadford Station, before I saw my good Marrable; I made myself surer afterwards when I called at the Station Hotel and heard how Mr. Belfield had arrived by the midnight train, and had ordered a fly to take him to the Abbey, how pleasantly he had chatted in the bar while the fly was being got ready, and how he had dismissed the carriage half-way down the avenue, preferring to walk the rest of the way.

"This was point number two in my case. It was clear that Mr. Belfield had made a secret visit to the Abbey after midnight, at a time when he was supposed to be at York or in Paris.

"The next thing was to discover how he contrived to disappear from the neighbourhood without having been observed at Chadford Station. I had found a fairly intelligent porter and a worthy station-master at that station, and from these two I had satisfied myself that neither Mr. Belfield nor his wife had left Chadford by train, up or down the line, after the night of August the 19th.

"To discover Mr. Belfield's manner of getting away from the neighbourhood cost me some time; but eventually I traced him to Bideford, where he must have gone on foot, a thirty-mile walk, and where at three o'clock on the afternoon of August 20th he chartered a sailing boat, in which he went round the coast to Bude, where he dismissed the boat. I took the trouble to go to Bude, and heard of him there, where he was out fishing all day, the innkeeper told me, and seemed strange in his manner. He stayed only four days, and then left in the coach for Launceston. He was not known at Bude by name, and he had no luggage, except a new night-shirt, brush and comb, which he had evidently bought on his arrival. The day on which he left Bude was the date which Mrs. Marrable had mentioned for his return from the supposed visit to Paris. The Bideford boatman described him as dead beat when he chartered the boat. He laid himself down at the bottom of the stern, on an old rug, and slept till sunset, but it was a very disturbed sleep, and the boatman thought he had something on his mind. They were coasting for nearly three days, the wind being against them part of the time, and the gentleman hardly ate anything, but finished a bottle of brandy which had been got for him at Bideford.

"What did this look like except the conduct of a criminal? Then comes his arrival at the Abbey, and the lie about a visit to Paris.

"Having got as far as this, I had not the slightest doubt that there had been a crime committed at the Abbey that night, or, in plain words, that Mr. Belfield murdered his wife. He got wind of her falsehood somehow, came home, and taxed her with it—there was a row, and he killed her. But how he killed her, and how he disposed of the body, are two questions which I have yet to solve."

Colonel Deverill groaned aloud, as he sat leaning forward in his chair, but he did not utter a word.

"He may have hidden her somewhere in that great barrack of a house," said St. Austell, "or he may have buried her in the garden."

"It would not be easy to hide a corpse in the largest house; nor easy to dig a grave between midnight and morning in the summer time, such a grave as should not be obvious to every eye. The one safe hiding-place would be the river; but that is more than a quarter of a mile from the house, at the nearest point."

"Why not drag the river?" asked St. Austell.

"I mean to get it done; but your lordship must remember that it is only within the last few days I succeeded in finding the Bideford boatman, and that it was his description of his passenger's appearance and conduct which confirmed my suspicion of foul play. There is such a thing as instinct; but one must have some better justification than instinct before taking active steps in a business of this kind."

"It is the fault of your tribe," said St. Austell. "You are all over-cautious. This man bears the brand of Cain on his forehead."

"You are right there. He has the criminal manner distinctly marked. I saw that when I spent an evening in his mother's house, and I was almost as certain then as I am now that he made away with his wife."

"When can we get the river dragged?" asked the Colonel.

"To-morrow at daybreak," answered Melnotte. "I have engaged a couple of men to do it. They know *what* they are to search for, but they will keep their counsel, and tell any curious inquirers that I dropped a valuable watch into the stream yesterday afternoon when I was rowing. I hired a boat at the bridge yesterday and rowed up the Chad and along the Abbey river; and in this place, where everything is known that concerns other people's business, that fact is sure to be known. The men will begin to drag at a point that I shall indicate to them nearest to the Abbey, and work down stream for a quarter of a mile—then go back to the same point and work up stream. If the body was thrown into the river, it will be found within those limits."

"What if that final evidence be found? The murderer will have had time to get out of reach of justice before a coroner's inquest can bring his crime to light," said St. Austell.

" He will not leave the country very easily. All the principal ports are being watched."

" But what of the smaller ports? He will get away, if he wants to escape."

" I don't believe he intends flight," said the Colonel. " Sir Adrian's manner was natural enough this afternoon when he talked of his brother having gone up to town, and the possibility of his travelling sooner or later. He has held his ground so long that I see no reason why he should take fright now."

" Unless he smells a rat and suspects Melnotte," said St. Austell.

The late winter dawn found St. Austell awake, in his old-fashioned four-post bed at the hotel by Chadford Bridge. He had been tossing about all night, sleepless, save for brief snatches of half-unconsciousness, which were rather waking dreams than sleep. Not for one instant of that weary night had Helen's image been absent from his thoughts. Again, and again, and again he had lived over their last meeting—recalling her looks and tones—her reluctant yielding to his prayers—and then her final promise, solemnly given, that she would be his.

He remembered how he had stood by her side with her hand clasped in his, and had said to her: "This promise makes you mine for ever, love. There must be no going back from your words to-day. To me it is a pledge as solemn as was ever made before the altar. May the worst evil happen to me if I ever fall away from my fidelity to you."

He had spoken in good faith; and now in his despair he told himself that this was the crowning love of his life, and that if she had lived he would have been true to her to the end.

"She was beautiful enough to enslave a man for a lifetime," he said to himself. "She had spirit enough to make her a difficult conquest; she was just clever enough to be a delightful companion for a clever man. She was the one perfect woman whom I have known."

He rose at daybreak, worn out by sleeplessness, and tried to refresh himself with an ice-cold bath. The house was early astir in the hunting season, and there was a great cry for baths and boots, and a hurrying to and fro of chambermaids in the corridor, by the time St. Austell was dressed. His breakfast was ready in the pretty sitting-room looking on to the road and the river at eight o'clock, but he was no better able to eat than he had been to sleep. He sat staring at the fire, and sipping a cup of tea, while he pictured to himself what the men were doing in the Abbey river.

He had intended to be down there at daybreak and to watch them at their work from the beginning. He had thought about it all night; but when the morning light came, his courage failed him. It was all too ghastly. How would death have used her, his beloved, she whose smile was to have been his Aurora, who was to have looked upon him in the happy dawn, in the glad beginning of each new day? How would she have fared in that cold couch where they were seeking her?   For the first time since his boyhood he prayed with all the strength and fervour of a believer—forgetting his scepticism, his sociology, his pessimism — everything, except the mental agony which wrung that prayer from him.   He prayed that the men with the drags might not find her.   That she might still be living—lost to him, perhaps, but living and lovely as she had been when last he looked upon her face.

The men must have been at work for more than an hour by this time, and it would take him nearly an hour to walk to the Abbey river; yet still he sat idly staring at the fire, hesitating, reluctant to face the result of that loathsome work.   At last, with an effort, he rose from his arm-chair, put on his coat, and went out.

There were three young men starting for a distant meet as he left the hotel.   They went clattering over the bridge, lighting their cigars, and talking and laughing, full of inane jocosity, as it seemed to St. Austell.   He almost hoped that one of them would be killed before they came back in the evening.   He execrated them for their mirthful ineptitude, as they went jogging up the stony hill, slapping their horses' haunches and swaggering in their saddles. He was glad to get away from the old English town, and its fringe of modern villas, to the lonely high road, and then to the footpath across the park, to that tributary of the Chad which was called the Abbey river, a stream in which many a fat and placid lay-brother had fished with net or line, and placed his eel-baskets, in the good old monkish days. St. Austell went down into the deep glen through which the river ran, parallel with the railroad. He went by the same narrow path which he had trodden last August, under the heavy summer foliage. Now the boughs were bare, and the winter sky looked coldly blue behind the dark tracery of leafless twigs. He saw the scene as in a dream, the wind-swept hillocks and hollows, the great brown trunks of the oaks, and in the distance the bright river glancing here and there across an opening in the woodland. He went down to the path where he had met Mrs. Baddeley yesterday afternoon. There was no one in sight, nor could he hear the sound of the irons scraping along the pebble bed. If the men were still at work, they were out of earshot. He walked slowly along, hoping that all was over, and that nothing had been found ; but a little further on he met Melnotte, and the first glance at his face told St. Austell that there had been a ghastly discovery.

"What are you doing here, Lord St. Austell?" said Melnotte hurriedly. "Pray go back. The worst has happened, and you ought not to be seen here. It may do you harm by-and-by. Take my advice and get away from this neighbourhood as soon as you can."

"What have they found? Where?" asked St Austell, ignoring his advice.

"They have found a body in a deep pool further down the stream; it is her's—there are ample means of recognition. The long brown hair, a wedding ring and keeper, a Persian rug wound round with a silk handkerchief. If her murderer had taken pains to secure her identification, and to show that she did not throw herself into the river, but was thrown in by somebody else, he could not have done more. Yes, it is very sad, my lord," as if in answer to the agony in St. Austell's countenance, "but there is no help. It is all over and done with. It is only what I expected. What you have to do is to get away from Chadford before the inquest, and to keep your name out of the business, if you can. You are known to have been with her on the last day of her life, to have planned an elopement with her. You may be suspected of her murder—who knows?"

"I don't care whether I am or not. Where is she? Let me see her," said St. Austell, trying to pass Melnotte, who contrived to block the path.

"For God's sake don't go that way. The men are carrying their burden to the dead-house. Let no.one who loved her look upon her—let no one but the surgeon see all that death and the river have left of poor humanity. Come back to Chadford with me, Lord St. Austell. I am going to the Coroner."

"What of her murderer? Is he to escape you?"

"Not if I can help it. I shall telegraph to Scotland Yard before I see the Coroner; and when I have seen him I shall get a magistrate's warrant for Mr. Belfield's arrest, and I shall take the first train for London with the warrant in my pocket."

"Sir Adrian will have communicated with his brother in the meantime, perhaps. Does he know what has happened?"

"Not yet, I think. There was no one down by the river while the men were at work except a gamekeeper, and I told him my story of having dropped my watch into the stream, which he seemed to swallow easily enough. I don't think Sir Adrian can have heard anything yet; but there will be plenty of talk, I suppose, when the remains have been taken to the dead-house."

Lord St. Austell looked back along the river path. He saw the men in the distance carrying their burden on a light hand-bier, which they must have taken with them from the dead-house, in expectation of this ghastly result. The burden was covered with a tarpaulin, and they were walking slowly in the same direction as St. Austell and Melnotte, only a good way behind.

He made no further attempt to see what lay beneath yonder gruesome covering; indeed he felt that Melnotte was right, and that he would not for worlds have looked upon those poor relics of all that he had loved. Let not that horrible image come between him and his memory of her fresh young beauty: let him not be reminded through her of what he himself must be—of humanity's common doom. He walked back to the town almost in silence, and left the detective to do his work alone. Melnotte suggested that he should go to the cottage and break the news to Colonel Deverill; but this St. Austell refused.

"I can help no man to bear his burden," he said; "my own is too heavy for me."

It was part of his burden to know that his unholy love had been the cause of Helen Belfield's death. If her husband was the murderer it was her lover who had brought about the crime.

CHAPTER XI.

VALENTINE BELFIELD did not go to the Great
Western Hotel after he left the house in Lisson
Grove. He was too deeply agitated to go quietly
back to his hotel, and eat a good supper and drink
a bottle of wine and go to bed and rest. He knew
that sleep was impossible, unless he could bring it
about by sheer fatigue, as he had done when he
walked from the Abbey to Bideford and had slept
the sleep of exhaustion in the bottom of the little
sailing boat. His only chance to-night was to walk
down the demon of restlessness that was in him;
so he turned his face northward and walked to
Hampstead, and then struck off towards Finchley
and Hendon, and roamed about among fields and
lanes all night, and at seven o'clock breakfasted at
a little public-house by the side of a canal, somewhere between Finchley Road and Child's Hill. It

was a house chiefly affected by bargemen, and nobody took any particular notice of him, the barmaid merely remarking that in all probability he was a swell who had been on the drink last night, and had been walking about to sober himself. He was sober enough this morning evidently, and was proof against all the barmaid's blandishments, though she took her hair out of papers before she carried him his breakfast of eggs and bacon and strong tea.

He had eaten nothing yesterday except the dainty little plate of bread and butter supplied by Madge, and he was faint and sick from the unaccustomed fast.

He fell asleep by the fire in the public-house parlour, slept through the entrances and exits of several relays of bargemen, slept amidst the odour of beer and the jingle of pewter pots, dozed on till the afternoon, and then paid his score and went away. He walked across the fields to the Edgware Road, and thence to Lisson Grove, where he went into a slopseller's shop and bought a suit of such clothes as are worn by the lower order of working men—an Oxford shirt, corduroy trousers, fustian jacket, and hob-nailed boots. He changed his clothes on the premises, and reappeared in Lisson Grove in corduroy and fustian, leaving his own things to be kept till called for. The shopman wondered not a little at this transformation.

" It's a lark, sir, I suppose ? " he said.

" Yes, it's a lark," answered Mr. Belfield, as he walked out of the shop.

" Well, I must say that I never laid eyes on a less larky-looking gent to be up to such a move as that," said the young. Israelite to his fellow-shopman, as he put Mr. Belfield's clothes away.

" There's a lady at the bottom of it, I make no doubt, Benjamin," replied the other, dismissing the subject, which remark was more accurate than speculative observations are wont to be.

It was dusk when Mr. Belfield rang the bell at the Forlorn Hope. Madge opened the door and did not recognize him, as he stood facing her silently, with his back to the light.

" What do you want, my good man ? "

"I want to be your servant, as I told you last night."

"Mr. Belfield, why are you still hanging about here?" cried Madge, in an agonized tone. "This is sheer madness."

"I believe it is next door to madness," answered Valentine, following her into the parlour, "but it is madness that only you can cure. There's no use in my going abroad, Madge, without you. I should only carry my guilty conscience and my misery with me; go where I might—Africa, Asia, the North Pole—it would be all the same to me. There is no place so strange, no life so full of danger, excitement, occupation, that would make me forget. You have the power to comfort me. You have the power to lay the ghost that haunts me. You alone can tell me that I have repented and have expiated my sin. You have the faith that moves mountains, and by your faith I may be saved. Leave me to myself and I shall perish inevitably. There is no help, no cure, but through you."

"You are mad," she said. "Yes, it is all madness. I have a good work to do here, and I cannot leave it."

" Let me stay here then, and work for you. That is what I have come for : to be your drudge, your slave; to be what Caliban was to Prospero. I am dressed for the part, you see. You will find how handy I can make myself, cleaning windows and scrubbing flag-stones, doing work that you and the sisters cannot do, with all your willingness to toil. And in bad cases, when a patient wants watching at night, I can do my part as a watch-dog. You don't know what I can be under your transforming power. Madge, I have no friend in the world but you."

" You have your mother, a nearer and dearer friend."

" No. To my mother my life has been a lie. She only is my friend who knows my sin and my repentance. Let me stay here, Madge, and when I leave the country, go with me as my guardian angel and my wife. Test the truth of my repentance, if you will, before you trust me. See how changed a creature I have become : how all that is vilest in my nature has been burnt out of it in the furnace of remorse. Test me to the uttermost as your servant, before you accept me as your husband."

Madge began to waver. He who was pleading to her knew not how urgently her own heart was pleading for him, how fondly she loved him, even in his degradation, stained with the shedding of blood.

"I believe it would be for your own safety to leave England instantly," she said. "There is no knowing what danger may arise. But if you are bent upon staying in this house and helping us in our work, I will talk to the sisters and see what can be done. Our fortnightly committee meeting will be held to-morrow afternoon, and most of the sisters will be here. If they consent to your being employed here—as a servant—I have no objection. There is a little room on this floor at the end of the passage, which you might have as a bed-room. It is small and rather dark, but it is dry and well ventilated."

"Give me any dog-hole," said Valentine. "Do you think I care how I am lodged? I want to be near you, Madge. I want to feel the support of your presence. That is all I ask."

" You must not call me Madge here. I am Sister Margaret.

" You shall be Sister Margaret, until you are wife Margaret. And now order me about, let me begin my slavery. Give me any work there is to be done."

" I don't think there is anything you can do to-night, but you shall clean all the windows to-morrow, if you like. Our windows have always been an affliction to me. We have done our best, but women are not good as window-cleaners. To-night you can take a holiday, but on future evenings we can give you some penmanship to do for us, letters to charitable people who help us. What must we call you, by-the-by ? You have a second Christian name, I think !"

" Yes. I was christened John Valentine, but I was always called by the second name, because my mother preferred it."

" Then here we will call you John."

She began to prepare the tea, as she had done on the previous evening, and two of the sisters came in to fetch the trays for their patients. One was an elderly woman, the other a girl of two-and-twenty, a pale gentle-looking creature, with a wistful expression in her large blue eyes.

Madge introduced Valentine to them as Mr. John, a person who in the outside world had been a gentleman, but who offered himself to them as a servant.

"If all the sisters approve, I think we may keep him here and find him very useful," she said. "At any rate he will stay here for to-night, and he can help you both in carrying round the coal-scuttles after tea."

Sister Agnes, the fair girl, sat down to tea with Madge and Valentine. She had a nervous manner, and spoke rarely, but Valentine was interested in her appearance, and inquired her history by-and-by, when she had gone back to her duties on the upper floor.

"Her's is a sad story. She belongs to wealthy people, and three years ago her life was a round of gaiety. She fell in love with an army doctor, and her family were all opposed to the match, and made her break off her engagement. He went to Egypt and was killed in the Soudan. She heard of his death unexpectedly from her partner at a dance, and for six months afterwards she was out of her mind. When she recovered, nothing would induce her to resume her old life of fine clothes and parties, nothing would induce her to hear of another lover. She devotes her life to charitable work, and all the money her father gives her is given to the poor. He is very liberal to her, although he disapproves of her way of life. She spends only one day of every week in this house, but she works for us out of doors, going about the streets at night, and talking to wretched women whom few girls of her age would have the courage to approach. That fragile looking girl has penetrated the darkest alleys about Clare Market, the most dangerous streets in Ratcliff Highway, where even the police go at the risk of their lives. She has never suffered any harm, has hardly ever been insulted by a coarse word. She has done more good than any other member of our sisterhood, although all have worked well."

"She can take your place when you have gone to the other side of the world, Madge."

Madge shook her head, with a sad, serious look, full of pity.

"I shall never leave my work, Mr. Belfield. I have given myself to it as much as if I had taken a vow. I am very sorry for you, I would do much to befriend you or to be of use to you, but I have put my hand to the plough, and I shall never take it away."

Valentine got up and began to pace the room, fuming.

"It is madness," he exclaimed; "a woman's craze. Only a woman would ever think of such a thing. Are there not hospitals for sick women?"

"There are hospitals for disease, but there are no hospitals for the weak and ailing, there are very few refuges for fainting sinners. There are plenty of orphanages for the spotless children, but there are few havens for the girls lost in the dawn of girlhood. Christ loved the innocent children and called them to his knees; but he had inexhaustible pity for the fallen women."

"So be it. You have set the ball rolling. You have begun the work. Others can carry it on."

"I will not leave it to others."

"You can continue your good work in the Antipodes. You will find sin in the New World as well as in the Old. There is no colony so recently founded that Satan has not helped to people it. Come, Madge, be reasonable. Three years ago you spurned me because I dared to approach you as a seducer. You did well, and I deserved your contempt. Now I come to you in all honour; I offer you all I have to give—my name, my life, my fortune, such as it is. I am to inherit all my mother's property, and I shall not be a poor man. I come to you with a blemished life, stained with one hour of darkest sin. But I am not altogether vile. I have repented that fatal hour in the long agony of months. I shall repent it all my life. Only you can make that life tolerable; only you can heal my wounds. Be my wife, Madge; take me with all my sins."

She held out her hand to him as he stopped in his pacing to and fro, and they remained for some moments silent, with clasped hands, he looking down at her, his eyes kindling as he looked; she very pale and her lips slightly tremulous.

"You love me, Madge," he said breathlessly; "you can forget all for my sake."

"I am very sorry for you," she answered softly, "but I have done with individual love. I have given my heart and life to my sorrowing sisters."

"It is a craze, Madge; I say again it is a craze."

"You have not seen the good done—you have not seen the altered faces. There are women now in happy honest homes whom we have picked up out of the gutter. If you were to see one young wife I know of, with her husband and her baby, you would not believe there had ever been a stain on her life. He took her, knowing what her past had been, and he has cherished her as a pearl of price. These are rare cases; but they are bright spots which cheer us and help us through many difficulties."

"Well, you are resolute, I suppose. You will go on helping strangers, and you will abandon me to my fate."

"I do not abandon you. I will do anything in my power to befriend you, short of sacrificing duty for your sake. I think you are very unwise to loiter here when you ought to be getting far away from England, losing your identity in a strange world. Your wife's relations will not be satisfied for ever without certain knowledge of her fate. An investigation may be set on foot at any moment, and the truth may be brought to light. You should be out of the way before that can happen."

" I tell you I do not value my life unless you will share it. I would rather stay here and clean windows, than riot in luxury at the Antipodes."

Madge answered nothing. She felt the hopelessness of the situation. He had chosen to come there, and she had not denied him shelter. She had taken upon herself in some wise the responsibility of his existence, since she had spoken of him to the Sisters ; and now she felt that his presence there would be a constant source of anxiety and mental disturbance. She would have to be perpetually on her guard, for ever denying a love which was the strongest passion of her life. It had been in her despair at resigning him, that

she had gone in quest of her erring mother. All
that she had done for others had been the oft-
shoot of her despairing love for him. And now
he offered himself to her in his desolation, and she
refused him.

"If I give way to his fancy he will forget all
the past, and his repentance will become a
mockery," she said to herself. "I cannot stand
in the place of his dead wife. I must not be a
gainer by his crime. How could I ever be at
peace, remembering that it was murder that set
him free to be my husband?"

CHAPTER XII.

" IS THERE NO BALM IN GILEAD ? "

THE Coroner was a portly gentleman of sixty-five, who had fulfilled all the duties of a general practitioner in Chadford and the surrounding villages for upwards of thirty years, and who had retired on a comfortable fortune, made partly by his profession, and partly by fortunate investments in modest little branches and loops of the great railway system, which time and traffic had developed into important lines. He had bought for himself an estate of forty odd acres of excellent pasture land between the Chad and the shoulder of the moor, and he had built for himself one of those essentially Philistine houses, of the streaky-bacon order, which are the delight of men who make their fortunes in country towns. Altogether, Mr. Mapleson was a very worthy person ; and when the office of Coroner became vacant his name appeared at the head of the poll.

Mr. Mapleson's study was a small square apartment, furnished with handsomely bound books of reference, a whip rack, and a formidable row of boots, which imparted an odour of Day and Martin to the atmosphere. Into this somewhat prosaic chamber, Melnotte, otherwise Markham, the detective, was ushered by the man-of-all-work on the morning of the discovery in the Abbey river; and in the briefest language he told what had happened, and his own conclusions therefrom.

" You think it is a case of murder," said Mr. Mapleson, biting the end of his pen.

" It can be nothing else. There is a carpet rolled round the body, and fastened with a silk handkerchief. Nothing has been touched since the remains were lifted out of the water; the colours in the carpet are distinguishable, and the string of silk round it is evidently a large neckkerchief. There can be very little doubt that the body was thrown into the water after death."

"The remains are not in a condition to be identified, I conclude."

"No. Time and the river have done their work of destruction only too well. There are other means of identification; wedding-ring and keeper for instance. The remains have not been touched more than was absolutely necessary in carrying them from the river to the dead-house, where they are waiting for the medical examination."

"And you are in a position to affirm that this is the body of Mrs. Belfield?"

"I am in a position to affirm as much, and I hope to be able to prove by circumstantial evidence that her husband murdered her, and threw her dead body into the river in the early morning of the 20th of August. But I will not trouble you with any further details. The inquest, which you are to hold to-morrow, will, I hope, be adjourned so as to give time for investigation. All I have done hitherto has been done in the dark. Many more details will doubtless come to light when the fact of the murder has been made public."

"Poor Lady Belfield!" sighed the Coroner. " Do you know that I had the honour of attending the family at the Abbey for thirty years. I remember the present Lady Belfield when her husband brought her home as a bride. She was a lovely woman then. She is a lovely woman now, lovely in mind as well as in person. This business will break her heart."

" I fear it will go hard with her."

" She adores her younger son. I have seen her agony when he has been laid up with some childish ailment. All her world was in that sick bed. And to see him accused of murder! Mr. Markham, if you are deluded, if you have not ample justification for the course you are taking, you will be much to blame."

" My justification will be shown at the inquest. There must be an inquest."

" Yes, that is inevitable. I wish, with all my heart, Mr. Markham, you had never had that river dragged."

" Then you would have had an undetected murderer in your midst."

" Better that perhaps, than that a good woman's heart should be broken."

It was a quality of Lady Belfield's character to evoke strong sympathy from all who were brought in familiar contact with her.

Melnotte had a fly waiting for him at the Coroner's door, and drove straight to the nearest Magistrate, from whom, after an interview of some length, he obtained a warrant for the arrest of Valentine Belfield on a suspicion of murder. With the County Magistrate, as with the Coroner, Melnotte found that sympathy with Lady Belfield was stronger than the abstract love of justice. He only just succeeded in getting the warrant signed in time for him to catch the next train for Exeter.

He was at Paddington at dusk, and went at once to the Great Western Hotel, where he inquired for Mr. Belfield.

Nothing had been seen of that gentleman except his luggage. That had been brought by a Great Western porter two evenings before with an intimation that Mr. Belfield was coming on to the hotel soon after; but nothing more had been heard of

him. Three large portmanteaux, a gun case, a roll
of rugs and coats, and a hat-box, all marked V.B.,
were stacked in the hall, pending the arrival of the
owner.

"Does Mr. Belfield usually stay here when he
comes to town?" asked the detective.

"Yes, for a night or two at a time. He is one
of our old customers," replied the manager.

Melnotte was at fault. That Valentine Belfield
should have brought all that luggage to London,
and then left England without it, seemed unlikely.
No purpose could have been served by bringing the
luggage unless for his use. To bring it to London
and abandon it at an hotel could in no manner assist
him in his flight, or tend to the mystification of his
pursuers. The only explanation seemed that he
had left his property at the hotel while he remained
in a state of uncertainty as to his future course.
He might be knocking about London. hesitating
as to whither he should bend his steps.

That he was in hiding anywhere was unlikely,
since he could as yet have no more cause for fear
than at any time since the commission of his crime.

Arguing with himself thus, Melnotte supposed that he would have very little difficulty in putting his hand upon the missing man.   He went straight from the Great Western to Scotland Yard, secured an assistant official, engaged a hansom by the hour, and started upon his quest.

" London is a big place, Redway," he said, " but the big London is only an aggregate of little Londons.   Each man has his own peculiar metropolis, which is generally no bigger than a moderate-sized country town.   Now I take it that Mr. Belfield's London is bounded on the West by Tattersall's, and on the East by the Criterion, on the South by Pall Mall, and by Oxford Street on the North.   If we don't find him within those limits we must look for him at Liverpool, Southampton, or Plymouth."

This was on the way to the Badminton, where Melnotte alighted and interviewed the porter. Mr. Belfield had not been seen there for six months.

"Not since Lord St. Austell's 'oss Postcard lost the Great Ebor," said the porter, who dated most events by the Racing Calendar.

From the Badminton, Melnotte drove to the Argus.

Here again Mr. Belfield had not been seen for months.

Melnotte drove westward, and contrived to see one of the men at Tattersall's, though the yard was shut.

No tidings of Mr. Belfield.

"That'll do for to-night, Redway," said Melnotte, considerably disconcerted. "I'll drive you back to the Yard, and then I'll go and dine and turn in for the night. If Mr. Belfield had been knocking about town in an open, easy-going manner, I believe I should have heard of him at one of those places. So I am disposed to think he has taken the alarm and is trying to get out of the country. I hardly think he can have got clear off yet; but I shall set the wires at work again before I eat my chop."

Mr. Melnotte set the wires at work to a considerable extent just before the closing of the chief telegraph office. He telegraphed to all the ports from which a man seeking to escape from justice was likely to attempt a start, and took measures to secure attention for the fugitive.

He was up and about betimes next morning, saw Mr. Belfield's tailor, took a stroll and an early cigar in the neighbourhood of Hyde Park Corner, hung about Tattersall's for an hour, looked in at a famous spurrier's in Piccadilly and a fashionable maker of hunting boots in Bond Street, and before eleven o'clock had satisfied himself that Mr. Belfield had not been seen at the West End of London since the previous summer.

The question to be solved was what had become of Mr. Belfield after he arrived at Paddington?

In such a town as Chadford the finding of a body in the Abbey river, and the notice of an impending inquest at the Ring of Bells Tavern in Little George Street, were not likely to remain unknown to the inhabitants. Before Melnotte had gone far upon his journey to London everybody in Chadford knew that a body was lying in the dead-house, and that an inquest was to be held upon the following afternoon.

Melnotte had imposed silence upon the men who dragged the river, and yet it was known somehow that there were appearances about the body that pointed to foul play rather than accidental drowning, while there were those who declared that the murdered corpse was that of the missing Mrs. Belfield.

Mr. Rockstone was one of the first to hear of the event which everybody in Chadford was talking about. He came out of the house of a sick parishioner, where all was quiet and shadow, into the bright winter sunlight, to find a group of townspeople standing in front of the saddler's shop in earnest conversation. From them he heard what had been found in the Abbey river.

His heart turned to lead as he listened. His mind had not been free from anxiety about Valentine's wife. He had carefully avoided questioning Lady Belfield or her sons, but he had wondered at the prevailing ignorance about the runaway wife's fate. When a woman elopes with a lover, there are generally those who know where she has gone, and who report and criticize her movements; but in this case no one had heard of the fugitive, no one knew where she was hiding her dishonoured existence. And now this finding of the corpse in the river pointed at fearful issues—at the best, suicide; at the worst, murder. He thought of Lady Belfield's agony when the talk of the town should reach her; and it must reach her very soon. In twenty-four hours every fact connected with the disfigured remains yonder must be brought to light, published to the world, discussed and commented upon in a tavern parlour. Friendship and love would be powerless to keep that horror from her, powerless even to blunt the edge of that anguish.

There was a fly crawling along the High Street on its return from the station. The Vicar jumped into it, and told the man to drive to the Abbey at his sharpest pace. He wanted to find Sir Adrian before anything was known there. Andrew ushered him into the library, where Adrian was sitting at his desk, surrounded with books and papers. He looked ill and careworn, the Vicar thought, but had too calm an air to have heard the evil news.

"My dear Rockstone, this is good of you," exclaimed Adrian, starting up and wheeling an arm-chair towards the hearth for his friend, and then seating himself opposite him. "It is an age since you have dropped in upon me so early. Tell me all your parish news, and your parish wants, if you have any."

"I cannot talk about the parish to-day. I have come to tell you of something terrible which has come to pass, and which may concern you and yours very nearly."

Adrian's face blanched to a ghastly pallor, and the hand grasping the arm of his chair trembled perceptibly.

"My God!" he gasped; "what is it?"

"A body has been found in the Abbey river an hour ago."

"How found—who found it?"

"The river was dragged this morning, I believe, at the instigation of Colonel Deverill's friend, Mr. Melnotte, who dropped his watch out of a boat a day or two ago, and wanted to have it found. A body has been found in the deep pool, near the chestnut copse, and there is to be an inquest to-morrow."

It was some moments before Adrian spoke, and then he asked quietly:

" Has the body been identified? "

" No, it is past all recognition, except by circumstantial evidence; but there is a rumour in Chadford, how arising I know not, that it is the body of your sister-in-law."

Again Adrian was silent.   He would have given worlds to be able to speak freely, to confess all the hideous truth to this one staunch friend, but loyalty to his brother restrained him.

" My sister-in-law's fate is wrapped in darkness," he said, after a long pause ; " I do not understand why any one should connect her with this drowned corpse."

" The reasons for such a suspicion will come to light at the inquest, I suppose. It is of your mother I have been thinking, Adrian, since I heard of this discovery.   How will it affect her? "

" How can it affect her?   I cannot see——" Adrian began helplessly.

" If it be found that there has been foul play."

" Why foul play ? Should this body be identified as that of Mrs. Belfield, the inference will be that she drowned herself."

" The people in Chadford are talking of something more terrible than that. There is a rumour that circumstances point to murder. Adrian, I must speak plainly," said the Vicar, with undisguised grief. " Suspicion points to your brother as the murderer. It is of your mother I think. What can you or I do to help her to bear the blow ? "

" Nothing, I fear. She adores Valentine. If any evil befall him it will kill her."

" You will do all you can to keep idle rumours from her, and yet to prepare her for anything that may happen to-morrow. Where is your brother ? "

" In London, I believe."

" You do not even know his whereabouts ? "

" No. He left here with the idea of going abroad—perhaps to Africa or South America. It was not his own fancy. My mother and I were anxious about his health and spirits, and urged him to travel. He has not written to me since he left."

" That is unlucky. He ought to be here to face any difficulty that may arise to-morrow."

Adrian was silent. To him, who knew all, the one hope was that his brother might have left the country for ever.

" Well, my dear Adrian," said the Vicar quietly, " we must wait and see what to-morrow will bring forth. I think you know that you may count upon me to do anything that lies within the compass of my will or my strength. Would to God I could see my way to being useful to you and your dear mother. I shrink from asking you questions, because I feel I am on delicate ground : but if—if you know anything that could assure me of the falsehood of these rumours—if, for instance, you had heard of your sister-in-law since her supposed elopement——"

" I have heard nothing of her. It is better that I should answer no questions till to-morrow. I suppose I shall be called at the inquest ?"

" I conclude so, if there is sufficient ground for identifying the body with your sister-in-law."

" Then I will keep my own counsel till I am before the Coroner."

Mr. Rockstone left Sir Adrian soon after this somewhat mystified by his calmness.

CHAPTER XIII.

THE inquest has been called for two o'clock in the afternoon, which hour gave the detective time to get back from London shortly after the opening of the inquiry.

The Coroner held his court in an upstairs room of the Ring of Bells. It was a wainscoted apartment, which at ordinary times was divided into two rooms, but which in its double length was used for vestry dinners, auctions, and public meetings of all kinds.

Colonel Deverill and Lord St. Austell sat near the Coroner, with their faces shadowed, and their figures partly hidden from the crowd at the lower end of the room by an old-fashioned four-fold screen. To the right of the Coroner sat a middle-aged, sandy-whiskered gentleman, with a bald head, and a legal air, who took careful notes of the proccedings. It was known to some of the audience that this gentleman was a solicitor from the Treasury, and that he was present in the capacity of Public Prosecutor; but it was not known to anybody that his arrival on the scene was brought about by Lord St. Austell's urgent application to the authorities at the Home Office.

Lady Belfield and Sir Adrian sat together on the other side of the room, and Lady Belfield's old and trusted lawyer, Mr. Gresham, of the old-established firm of Gresham, Gresham, and Thorogood, Lincoln's Inn, sat a little way in front of his client. Adrian had entreated his mother not to be present at this inquiry; but she had insisted, and he could but submit to her will. She was pale as marble, and her plain black gown and bonnet made her pallor more conspicuous. Her old friend the Vicar sat just behind her, and bent forward now and then to speak to her. On the table in front of the Coroner and Jury lay the stained and ragged remains of a Persian prayer-rug, a silk muffler, and four rings.

Felix Loseby, a medical practitioner of Chadford, was the first witness.

He deposed to having examined the body, which he pronounced to be that of a young woman with long brown hair. He had discovered an injury upon the left temple, where the bone was fractured as if by a heavy blow from some blunt instrument. Such a blow, he said, in answer to the Coroner's question, would be sufficient to cause death. There was no other mark of violence.

The Coroner asked if death could have been caused by drowning.

No. The state of the lungs indicated that the deceased had died before she was thrown into the water.

The rings on the table had been found on the fingers of the left hand, which was so confined by the carpet and the long hair, that it was impossible for the rings to have been washed off by the action of the water.

He was of opinion that the body had been in the river for some months; probably, in reply to a juryman, six months.

Mr. Loseby further described how the rug had been tied round the body by the long silk muffler now lying on the table.

The two men who had dragged the river deposed to having found the body in a deep pool, which formed a little inlet, under a group of willows.

Colonel Deverill was next examined. He had seen the remains, and believed them to be those of his daughter, on account of the colour and texture of the hair. His daughter had been remarkable for the beauty and profusion of her hair, which was of a peculiar shade of brown, with a natural ripple in it. He could swear to the cat's eye and diamond ring upon the table as his daughter's engagement ring, given to her by Mr. Belfield. He could swear to the ring with a brilliant cross set in black enamel. It was a mourning ring, and his own gift to his younger daughter. It contained her mother's hair.

The Colonel was deeply affected while giving his evidence, and Lady Belfield seemed equally overcome. There was a dead silence at the end of the room where the crowd was congregated—a silence of mournful sympathy.

Mr. Belfield was next called; whereupon Mr. Gresham rose and informed the Coroner that Mr. Belfield had gone to London three days before. A message had been telegraphed to him at the Great Western Hotel, where he usually put up, and to the two clubs which he was in the habit of using, but no reply had yet been received.

It was at this juncture that Melnotte quietly entered the room, and made his way to a seat at the back of the Coroner.

Sir Adrian Belfield was next called.

He was asked to state the circumstances of Mrs. Belfield's disappearance from the Abbey.

"I can only tell you that we rose one morning— on the morning of August the 20th—to find her gone."

"Did she leave no trace of the manner by which she had gone?"

"No. She left a letter stating her intention to leave her husband, which letter was found by a servant after my sister-in-law's disappearance."

"Can you produce that letter?"

"I cannot. It is in my brother's possession."

" You and Lady Belfield were both at the Abbey
at the time of Mrs. Belfield's disappearance, I
understand."

" We were."

" Do you know nothing as to the hour at which
she went, or her mode of leaving the house?"

" Nothing."

He answered unfalteringly. He knew that in
so answering he was guilty of perjury; but he
knew also that the only chance of saving his
brother was to lie unblushingly. He who loved
truth and honour better than his own life was
willing so to perjure himself for the love of his
brother, and of the heart-broken mother yonder,
whose sad eyes were watching him.

" Was Mr. Belfield at the Abbey on that night?"

" He was not."

" You are sure of that fact? You had better
reflect seriously, Sir Adrian, before you answer my
question."

He suspected an attempt to trap him into a
fatal admission, and answered deliberately :

" I am sure."

"That will do, Sir Adrian. You can sit down."

Melnotte whispered something to the Coroner, and the next witness was called. John Grange, coachman at the Station Hotel, Chadford Road.

"Do you remember anything particular happening upon the 19th of August last year?"

"Yes, sir. I remember being called up to take out a fly after eleven o'clock. There's a train comes into Chadford Road Station at 11.43, but we don't often get a fare by that train, as it's a slow 'un. I was to get my landau ready and look sharp about it, for Mr. Belfield."

"Where did you drive Mr. Belfield?"

"I took him as far as the avenoo leading to the Abbey. In the middle of the avenoo he puts out his 'ed and calls me to stop. and gets out of the trap a'most before I could stop. He gives me a shilling, and tells me to go home, and then he starts off a'most at a run terwards the Abbey."

"Are you quite sure as to the date?"

"Can't be no mistake about that. The fly was booked that night. There it is in the master's day-book. 'August 19th. Fly to Belfield Abbey.'"

" You are sure the gentleman you drove was Mr. Belfield ?"

" Quite sure."

" Would you know Mr. Belfield from his brother, Sir Adrian ?" asked Mr. Gresham, the Coroner having no further questions to ask this witness.

" Yes, sir. Mr. Belfield's a bigger-made man. I've known the two gentlemen by sight since they was boys, and I could swear to either of them anywheres."

So much for John Grange, of the Station Hotel.

Lady Belfield was the next witness called.

She was asked to state any facts she could recall connected with Mrs. Belfield's disappearance.

" There is very little for me to remember," she said. " My first knowledge of my daughter-in-law's disappearance was from my housekeeper, at nine o'clock in the morning. A housemaid had found Mrs. Belfield's room empty."

" A housemaid found her room empty in the morning of August 20th. Had the bed been slept in ? "

" It had not."

" Then the inference would be that she left the house at night."

" I do not know that. She may have remained up all night, and may have left early in the morning before the servants were up.

" She left a letter, I understand ? "

" Yes, the housemaid found a letter."

" Addressed to your son ? "

" It was written to my son."

" Was it a sealed letter ? "

" No, it was open and unfinished."

" An unfinished letter, left open ; lying on a table, I presume ? "

" I did not ask where the letter was found."

" Did you see your daughter-in-law's room that morning ? "

" No, I went to London by the morning train. A telegram was delivered just after I heard of my daughter-in-law's disappearance—a telegram purporting to come from my younger son in London, and which caused me considerable alarm. I started for the station as soon as my carriage could be got ready."

" Was the telegram actually from your son? "

" It was not.   I have reason to believe that it was part of a plot to decoy my daughter from her home."

" Did you find your son in London? "

" I did not."

" Had you any reason to suppose that he was in London? "

" Either there or at York.   I had heard of him last at York."

" You did not know that he came to the Abbey on the night of the 19th ? "

" I cannot believe that he was there."

" Yet you have heard the evidence of the man who drove him into your park? "

" I have heard that."

" What time did you and your family retire to rest on the 19th of August ? "

" Mrs Belfield left the drawing-room soon after nine o'clock. She complained of a headache. I went to my bed-room at half-past ten, and Sir Adrian went to the library at the same time."

" Did you hear anything unusual during the night?"

" Nothing."

" How far is your bed-room from that occupied by Mrs. Belfield?"

" It is at the other end of the house."

" You say Sir Adrian retired to the library at half-past ten upon that particular evening. Do you know at what hour he went to his bed-room?"

" It must have been very late. He is in the habit of reading late at night; and on this night he told me that he read later than usual, and fell asleep in his chair in the library."

" Do you mean that he did not go to bed at all?"

" He did not tell me that, only that he had fallen asleep in his chair."

The next witness was Jane Pook, the house-maid.

On being asked if she remembered anything particular upon the morning of August the 20th, she described her entrance into Mrs. Belfield's bed-room with the early cup of tea which that lady was in the habit of taking while her bath was being prepared for her; and how she had found the room empty, and the bed undisturbed; and how on looking about the room she had discovered an open letter lying on the floor.

"Did you read that letter?"

"Yes, I was so taken aback that I read the letter almost before I knew what I was doing. If I'd had time to give it a thought, I should have been above doing such a thing."

"Did anything peculiar strike you in the letter?"

"It was a dreadful letter, telling her husband that she did not love him, and that she loved somebody else, and was going off with him. The letter wasn't finished. It left off in the middle of a sentence."

"As if she had been interrupted while writing it?"

"Yes, sir."

"Did you observe anything else unusual on that particular morning?" inquired the sandy-whiskered gentleman, upon the Coroner's interrogatory being finished.

“ No, sir—nothing else, leastways——”

Jane Pook faltered, reddened, and looked nervously towards Sir Adrian.

“ There *was* something else,” said the sandy-whiskered gentleman. “ What was it ? ”

“ Sir Adrian’s bed had not been slept in.”

“ Where had Sir Adrian spent the night ? ”

“ He must have been all night in the library. The oil was burnt out in the two lamps, and the candles on his desk were burnt lower than usual. Sir Adrian often sits up late at night, studying.”

“ But does he often refrain from going to bed at all ? ” inquired the sandy-whiskered gentleman.

“ No, sir.”

“ Did you ever know such a thing to occur before ? ”

“ I can’t call to mind, sir.”

“ You mean that it never did occur before ? ”

“ I think not, sir.”

“ Have you lived long at Belfield Abbey ? ”

“ Five years.”

Mrs. Marrable, the housekeeper, was next called. She was very pa'e, and her eyelids were swollen with weeping. She gave a vindictive look at Mr. Melnotte, as she took the sacred volume in her hand, which argued ill for the Christian temper of her mind at that moment.

" Do you recognize anything upon that table ? " asked the Coroner.

" No, sir."

" Look again, if you please. There is something there which you have seen before. Perhaps you had better put on your spectacles, and look at the object a little closer. Do you see now what it is ? "

" It looks rather like an old rug."

" It *is* a rug. I think you have seen that rug before."

" I can't call it to mind."

" I fear you must have a bad memory, Mrs. Marrable. Did you ever miss a carpet or rug of any kind out of one of the Abbey bed-rooms ? "

Again Mrs. Marrable looked at Melnotte, the detective, and by the nervous action of her fingers it might be inferred that she longed to inflict some slight injury upon his imperturbable countenance.

"I may have been foolish enough to talk some of my nonsense to spies and eavesdroppers," she said acrimoniously, "but as to missing a rug or a carpet out of a house where there's nothing but honest servants——"

"Mrs. Marrable, was there or was there not a Persian rug missing out of Mrs. Belfield's bed-room on the 20th of August?" asked the sandy-whiskered gentleman severely. "Remember, if you please, that you are on your oath."

Mrs. Marrable hesitated, looked piteously at her mistress, whose face was rigid with agony, and replied:

"I did miss a Persian rug."

"Can you tell me the pattern of that rug?"

"It was something of a pine pattern."

"If you will be good enough to look closer at the rug on the table, I think you will see that it is a pine pattern."

"It is too much discoloured for me to make out anything about it."

"You are underrating your own intelligence. Pray look at the rug again. Now, will you swear that is not the rug you last saw in Mrs. Belfield's bed-room ?"

" No."

" Then perhaps you will admit that it is the same rug ? Remember that to deny a fact of which you are convinced is perjury."

" I believe it is the rug."

" That will do."

The winter day had closed in some time before the inquiry had arrived at this stage; and the Coroner now suggested the adjournment of the inquest, to give time for the development of fresh evidence.

" The case is exceptionally painful, gentlemen," he said, " and I should be sorry if anything were done in a hurried manner. I believe that upon every consideration it will be best that this inquiry should be adjourned until next Friday, when we will meet again in this room at the same hour as we met to-day. The interment of the remains of that unhappy lady whose fate we are here to investi-gate can be proceeded with in the meantime."

It was some time before the room was cleared of

coroner, jury, reporters, and audience, but Lady Belfield and her son did not wait for the crowd to disperse. They retired together by a door near the end of the room where they had been sitting, and thus escaped the crowd.

Sir Adrian put his mother's hand through his arm and supported her faltering footsteps as he led her downstairs and out into the dusky street, where her carriage was waiting for her. She spoke no word until after the carriage had moved away, and then at last the white lips moved, and she asked in tones that were like a wail of agony:

"Is this true, Adrian?"

"What, mother?"

"Is it true that he came to the Abbey that night?"

"Yes, it is true."

"Oh, God! And you swore that he was not there."

"I perjured myself—to save him. I knew nothing about the fly. I did not know that any one had seen him."

"You tried to save him—that means that he is

guilty—that—he killed her," sobbed Lady Belfield, in broken snatches of speech.

Adrian was silent for some moments, thinking deeply, deliberating within himself if it might be possible to keep the fatal truth from his mother. But it seemed to him that it would not be possible, that the meshes of the net were fast closing round him and his brother, that all which had been done that night in the darkness must inevitably be brought to light. The only hope left was that Valentine might escape pursuit.

" Mother, I have striven to keep this horror from you : I have sworn falsely this day in the hope that my brother's guilt might remain for ever hidden : but I feel that all is over, that the evidence you have heard must bring his guilt home to your mind as well as to the minds of strangers. Thank God he is not so guilty as he may appear ; he was not a deliberate murderer."

And then he told his mother briefly, plainly, unflinchingly, how the deed had been done; how one moment of passion had made Valentine Belfield a criminal; how he had obstinately insisted upon hiding his crime, and had thus brought upon himself the ignominy of this day's inquiry.

"How are we to save him, Adrian?" asked Lady Belfield. "We must save him. Oh God, to think of my son arraigned for murder, standing in the dock to answer with his life! They would hang him, Adrian—they would hang my beloved one. Oh, Adrian, you can help me to save him, to get him away to some safe hiding-place before the police can hunt him down. There are corners of the earth where he would be safe. I would go with him, live with him anywhere—in the dreariest spot of earth, among a savage people—happy and full of gratitude to God, only to know that my dearest had been saved from a shameful death."

"We will do all that ingenuity can do, dear mother," Adrian answered quietly, while his mother sat back in a corner of the carriage, her face hidden, her whole frame convulsed with grief. "In all probability Valentine has left England before now. The fact that he has not written to me may mean that he is on the sea; that he snatched the earliest opportunity of getting away."

The carriage was in the avenue by this time. As the coachman drew up his horses in front of the Abbey a gig drove rapidly round the gravel sweep, and pulled up a little way from the porch.

Two men alighted from the gig. One of them was Melnotte, the detective; and in the other Sir Adrian recognized a local police-officer.

He took no notice of the two men until he had assisted his mother into the house, and placed her in the care of her maid, who was waiting in the hall to receive her. Then he went back to the porch, and confronted the detective.

"I am sorry to appear upon an unpleasant errand, Sir Adrian" said Melnotte. "I have a warrant for your arrest as accessory to the murder of Mrs. Helen Belfield. It is too serious a charge to admit of bail, so I must request you to accompany me to Chadford without loss of time."

"You mean to Chadford Gaol, I suppose?"

"Yes. You will be treated there with all respect, and accommodated with a private room. I must warn you that anything you may say——"

"You may save yourself the trouble. I am not going to say anything, except that I consider that Colonel Deverill has been guilty of ungentlemanlike conduct in bringing a detective into my house as my guest."

"Colonel Deverill's position as a father may excuse some laxity in a point of etiquette."

"It was more than a point of etiquette; it was a point of honour, Mr. Melnotte—if your name is Melnotte."

"My name is Markham. I was a gentleman once upon a time, Sir Adrian. Necessity compels men to adopt strange trades. Will you be driven to the gaol in your carriage, sir, or will you allow me to drive you in my gig? Thompson can walk back."

"I may as well go in your gig. It is too dark for any one to recognize me; and, for the matter of that, everybody in Chadford will know where I am before to-morrow morning. Be good enough to wait while I give an order to my servant."

The detective waited, taking care not to let Sir Adrian out of his sight during the brief delay.

Adrian ordered a valise to be packed with the necessary changes for an absence of three or four days, and then sat down at a table in the hall to write to his mother, while Melnotte stood in front of the fire, warming his back and admiring the stately old panelled hall and vaulted roof.

It was a difficult letter to write, and Adrian could think of only one form of consolation. "My arrest may make my brother's escape easier," he wrote. "They cannot find any direct evidence against me, and, on reflection, I believe it will be impossible to bring any conclusive proof against Valentine. Put your trust in Providence, dear mother, and hope for the passing of the dark hour. My heart is less heavy than it was under the burden of an intolerable secret."

An hour later his mother was sitting by his side in the gloomy-looking parlour which he was privileged to occupy in Chadford Gaol.

"My poor Adrian, it is so hard that you should suffer—you, who are innocent—who would have saved your brother's good name had he only been guided by you. It is very hard."

"I can bear it, mother. Would to God it had been possible for me to pay the penalty of my brother's crime. I would have done as much willingly—for your sake."

CHAPTER XIV.

"I WILL STAND BY MY BROTHER."

IT was the morning after the inquest, and Valentine had begun his new occupation as man-of-all-work so soon as there was light enough in the dull grey sky to allow him to set about his labours. The sisters were astir at dawn, working diligently, lighting the fires, sweeping the stairs, and cleaning the lower rooms. Valentine relieved them of those rougher tasks which they had performed hitherto. He washed out the back yard, washed and hearth-stoned steps and window-sills, and cleaned all the lower windows. Inexperience made him clumsy; but energy and strength of will carried him through the work much better than could have been expected.

"I had no idea window-cleaning was such in-teresting work," he said to Madge, as she gave him his breakfast of tea and bread in the parlour, where she and the two sisters had breakfasted previously. Their morning fare was only dry bread. Butter was a luxury reserved for the evening. There was a wholesome meal of meat and vegetables at two o'clock. Tea was taken between five and six, after the inmates had been served; and there was a supper of bread and cheese at ten o'clock. The sisters who sat up with the sick were allowed tea and bread and butter in the course of the night, but neither wine nor beer was drunk by any of the sisterhood, and stimulants were only given to patients when ordered by the doctor.

Valentine took his tea and bread with as contented a spirit as if he had been in the centre of Africa, and no better fare had been possible.

"I'm afraid you will soon grow tired of window cleaning and of dry bread," said Madge, contemplating him with her grave slow smile, full of thought.

"You do not know me. If I am strong for evil, I may also be strong for good. I mean to serve you—as Caliban served Prospero, yet not like

Caliban. He served for fear; I am your slave for love. I shall be ready to clean the outsides of the upper windows as soon as I can begin without disturbing the patients. I am promised the loan of a ladder from your milkman round the corner."

"That milkman is a treasure. He keeps one particular cow for our consumptive patients, and though I believe he adulterates all the rest of his milk, our supply is always pure; and he charges us a halfpenny a quart less than other people pay. You cannot think how good people are to us."

"I'll go out and look after my ladder," said Valentine; and he walked off in a business-like manner, wearing his fustian and corduroy as if he had never worn anything else.

A few paces from the house he met a boy with newspapers, bought a *Daily Telegraph*, and put it into his pocket.

"For my dinner-hour's amusement," he said to himself. "I believe the working man always reserves the news for his dinner-hour."

His step, which had been so heavy and sluggish of late, in the monotonous leisure of his country home, was light to-day, as he went for the ladder. He came back carrying it on his shoulder. His experiences as a sportsman had braced his muscles, and he carried the ladder as easily as if it had been a gun or an oar. He felt nearer happiness than he had felt since that fatal night. In the first place, it was an infinite relief to be away from the scene of his crime; and in the second place, there was a world of comfort in being associated with the one woman whose influence could at once soothe and strengthen—the one woman who knew his ghastly secret, yet had not turned from him with loathing.

He could never forget that kiss upon his forehead which had assured him of a woman's pitying love. He had taken no base advantage of that sign of tenderness; he had not pressed his suit with the vehemence of a passion that will take no denial. He had been humble with her, as became him in the abasement of his guilt. And he was happier now, toiling for her, than he could have hoped to be. He laboured at his task all the morning, one of the sisters working with him on the inner side of the windows; and the general result was an increase of brightness which seemed like the forerunner of spring. He saw something of the inmates of the Forlorn Hope in the course of his morning's work. In the front room of the first floor—once a drawing-room, with French windows and an iron balcony—he saw several women of various ages, from eighteen to forty, some engaged in plain sewing, others in fancy needlework, and one at an ironing-board. These were the convalescents and those who had been received because of their destitution rather than on account of ill-health. In other rooms he saw the sick in white-curtained beds. Everywhere there were signs of careful management, cleanliness, inventive power, the ability to do much with little means. This humble institution, maintained by a few women, was more interesting than the grandest building which public charity ever raised.

By half-past one the windows were all cleaned, and Valentine went to the little room which had been allotted to him, the room where he had spent a sleepless night on a hard and narrow pallet, which the Iron Duke might have approved. Here he washed off the traces of his toil, brushed his fustian jacket, and prepared himself for dinner, hoping to eat that meal *tête-à-tête* with Madge. He had heard her say that the three sisters dined in the upper room with the women, and that she waited upon them. She must take her own dinner somewhere, he argued. Why not with him?

His hopes were strengthened on going into the parlour, where he saw the table laid for two. Madge was upstairs, where the dinner was going forward. It was she who carved and distributed the food, while the other three sisters ate with their charges, and maintained the cheerful tone of a family meal. There was nothing penitential in the atmosphere of everyday life at the Forlorn Hope: yet sorrow for sin was deeply felt there, and many a penitent's tears had been poured into the sisters' laps, and many a heart-broken sob had mixed with the prayers of the community.

Valentine seated himself by the window, and unfolded his *Telegraph*.

He began with a sweeping survey of the pages, to see what was best worth reading.

" A Devonshire Tragedy.

" Considerable excitement has been created at the town of Chadford, North Devon, by the finding of a body in the Abbey river near that town, under circumstances which appear to indicate foul play. The body has been identified as that of the wife of Mr. Belfield, of Belfield Abbey, Chadford, whose disappearance from her home was one of the social scandals of last autumn."

Here followed a full report of the Coroner's inquest, and an account of the arrest of Sir Adrian Belfield on suspicion of being concerned in the murder of his sister-in-law.

" The startling character of the revelations, the social position of the parties involved, and the respect which is felt for them in the neighbour-hood combine to render this one of the most extraordinary cases that have come before the public for many years, and the result of the adjourned inquest will be awaited with keen anxiety."

Slowly and deliberately Valentine Belfield read and pondered over the report of the inquest. To him who was in the secret the circumstances of his guilt seemed to start out into the broad light of day from the evidence of those different witnesses. The unfinished letter, broken off in the midst of a sentence—the missing rug found tied about the victim's body—his own secret visit to his mother's house—his brother's vigil: all pointed at the fact of murder.

Yet how, in the face of such evidence against him, had they dared to arrest his brother? Under suspicion of being concerned in the murder? Yes, he had been with the murderer in that dreadful hour after the deed was done. They two had been together, and the law might call Adrian an accessory after the fact.

He was still poring over the report, when Madge came in, carrying a tray with the fragments of the upstairs meal.

"Come, brother John," she said cheerily, as she

set a dish on the table. " My people were in very good appetite, but there is plenty left for you and me. I am sure you must be ready for dinner."

"Not quite," he answered gravely, "and I'm afraid I shall spoil your dinner if I tell you what has taken away my appetite."

She went over to him and laid her hand upon his shoulder, looking down at the newspaper. Her quick eye caught the familiar names, and she read the report of the inquest across his shoulder.

"You see I was right," she said; "there was not an hour to be lost, and you have wasted days. You will go at once now—at once—or as soon as it is dark. It may be safer not to leave this house till dusk. Your working-man's suit will serve a good purpose now. I will go out and get you an outfit, and pack everything ready for you. Then you must start for Liverpool by the train that leaves Euston at seven this evening, and you can get off to-morrow morning by any ship that may be leaving. There must be steamers leaving every day. Take the first that will carry you far away from England. You will go, won't you?"

He was holding her arm in his strong grasp, looking at her fixedly, yet hardly seeming to listen to her eager words.

" You will go ? " she urged.

" Not without you. I have said it before, Madge, and I say it again. I have no desire to prolong my life unless I can spend it with you."

" You have seen what my work is here, and you ask me to give it up in order to——"

" To share a murderer's exile; to play hide and seek with the law; to drive away the horrors of remorse; to cure bad dreams; and to save a sinner from madness. That is what I ask you to do, Madge. Any one can carry on your work here. No one but you can save me."

" What if I were to say yes ! " asked Madge, after a few moments of deepest thought, returning that fixed look of his with a gaze that was still more earnest, for it seemed to peer into his very soul.

" You lift me from hell to heaven at the mere thought. Oh, Madge be generous, reward an ungenerous lover. I lost you once by the meanness of my love. I love you now as you deserve to be loved. Forget all I have ever been : remember only what I am—your adoring slave. Let us be married before the Registrar to-morrow morning. We can start for Liverpool afterwards."

"And when we are gone, Valentine, when you have got clear away, what is to become of your brother ? Have you thought of that ? "

No, he had not thought of that ; but he answered, almost carelessly :

" He will be safe—there can be no evidence against him."

" The evidence against him is almost as strong as against you. There is no one but you who can prove his innocence."

" And you would have me give myself up in order to clear him."

" If there is no other way of clearing him— yes."

" You hold my life very lightly."

" I hold life as less than honour. You have brought your brother into peril. It would be a cowardly act to desert him now."

"Yet a few minutes ago you urged me to leave the country."

"I forgot all but your own safety."

"I have told you that I do not set a high price upon that. Well, you are right, Madge. You are always right. I will stand by my brother. I will go back to Chadford to-morrow, even if Chadford be a short cut to the gallows."

"It will not prove that," she answered, her pale face kindling with the light of enthusiasm. "Confess the truth as you confessed to me. Let all the world know how you sinned in one fatal moment of passion, and how you tried to hide your sin. There are few who will not pity you, as I pity you."

She bent over him as he sat leaning forward, with his eyes brooding upon the ground. She laid her hand upon his head, and, thrilled by that gentle touch, he looked up and their eyes met.

"Say that you love me, Madge, and I will do anything."

"Yes, I love you—yes, I always loved you. It was love for you that drove me out into the world in my despair, to find something to fill my empty heart, aching for love of you. It was love of you that sought relief in soothing sinners. I have always loved you. Do this one brave thing, and I can respect and honour you."

"Will you marry me, Madge, if Jack Ketch does not get me?"

"Yes."

"That is a promise worth waiting for. Will you wait for me, Madge, if they keep me in Dartmoor prison till my hair is white?"

"I will wait till the end of my days. Come what may, there shall be no other love in my life."

"Pledge yourself to that with a kiss, Madge."

He clasped his arms round her as she bent over him, and their lips met, half in sorrow, half in joy; joy on his side that she was won, would own love's subjection, she who had seemed to him too strong for love; sorrow on her side that he must stand as a criminal before his fellow men, and risk his life for honour's sake.

"When shall I start for Chadford, Madge?" he asked.

"The sooner the better. The police may be on the watch for you. I should like you to be able to return there as a free agent."

"You are right. It would be hateful to go back under convoy. There is an afternoon train, a beast of a train that stops at nearly every station, the train by which I travelled that night," with a shudder. "I will go by that."

"I will go with you."

"Madge," he cried, overjoyed.

"I may as well keep you company on the journey, while we are still free to be together. Will you go in those clothes?"

"No. They would look like a disguise. I left a suit at the slop-seller's. If any one would fetch it?"

"I will go for it," she answered, "and I will arrange for leaving this house for a few days."

CHAPTER XV.

THE police had not been idle during the day of the inquest, or during that day on which Valentine Belfield was making his first experiment in the art of window-cleaning. The usual machinery had been at work, and with the usual result of failure during the first forty-eight hours of pursuit. The first few days in such a hunt are generally blank.

Melnotte had not gone back to London after the inquest. He relied on subordinate intelligence, assisted by photography, to track the suspected criminal. His own work he felt lay in the neighbourhood of Chadford, where the final links in the chain of evidence were to be put together. Lord St. Austell was still at the Lamb Hotel, keeping very quiet, but ready at all seasons to confer with the detective.

Sir Adrian spent the first day of his imprisonment in a listless indifference as regarded himself or his own convenience, but in keenest anxiety about his brother. He had Mr. Gresham, the solicitor, with him upon the evening of his arrest, and they discussed the evidence given at the inquest.

" You have to deal with the evidence as it stands, Gresham," he said. " I admit nothing about myself or my brother."

" I am sorry to say, Sir Adrian, that unless you can disprove John Grange's statement, you tacitly confess yourself guilty of perjury."

" I am not in a position at present to disprove Grange's statement ; but I think I have as good a right to be believed as he has."

" On any indifferent matter your word would doubtless be taken in preference to his ; but on a question of life and death for your brother, the statement of any disinterested witness would be preferred to yours."

"What am I to do in my brother's interest? I do not care about myself."

"In both your interests we must try to secure Distin. I will telegraph to him directly the office is open to-morrow morning."

Mr. Distin's fame as a criminal lawyer was not unknown to Sir Adrian Belfield, and it seemed to him well that in this struggle with Fate he should have the best assistance that training and hereditary instinct could afford. Distin had been suckled upon criminal law, and cradled in the Old Bailey. No doubt Distin was the man.

It was a shock to Sir Adrian, therefore, when Mr. Gresham came into his room next morning—soon after the coffee and hot rolls which an obsequious official had brought over from the Ring of Bells—carrying Mr. Distin's telegram: "Sorry I cannot accept your retainer. Am already engaged by Colonel Deverill."

"This is unlucky for us, Sir Adrian. It is bad enough not to have Distin with us, but it is worse to have him against us."

"You can get some one else I suppose if you

are not strong enough yourself to protect our interests."

"I am not a criminal lawyer, Sir Adrian; but perhaps my regard for your family may stand in the place of experience at the Old Bailey. I am not afraid to undertake your defence, if you will trust me."

"I would rather trust you than any other member of your profession."

The following day was Sunday—a dismal Sabbath for Adrian, who had so rarely been absent from his place in the old parish church, and whose Sundays had been verily days of rest—days devoted to kindly visitings among the old and infirm, to serious reading and quiet thought. A gloom had overshadowed all his days since his brother's crime, but Sunday had been not the less a day apart—a time of prayer and meditation, remorseful memory of the hapless dead, and intercession for the sinner.

This day he spent with his mother sitting beside him, in mournful silence, or in silent prayer for the most part. They sat together through the

dull wintry day, taking very little heed of time—
only noting the passing of the hours by the church
bells, sounding with a heavy monotony from the
old Norman tower near at hand—the fine old square
tower, with its crocketed finials, rising high above
tiled roofs and picturesque gables, clustering on
the summit of the hilly street. More distant bells
came with a softer sound from a church on the
other side of the river, and, mingling with these,
came the shrill single bell of a Nonconformist con-
venticle. To that mourning mother's ear it seemed
as if the air were full of bells, and she thought,
shudderingly, of that great bell of St. Sepulchre's,
which she had read of tolling with funereal stroke
for the passing of a sinner's soul. The bells had
done their worst by seven o'clock in the evening,
when Adrian entreated his mother to share the
dinner that had been brought from the hotel for
him. She had ordered her carriage to come for
her at ten o'clock. They sat down at the shabby
little table, in the light of a paraffin lamp, and each
made a pretence of eating in the hope of encouraging
the other.

There was to be an inquiry before the Magistrates to-morrow—an inquiry at which Adrian would appear in his new character—no longer a witness, but a prisoner, accused of being implicated in his brother's crime.

The morning came, with a low grey sky and a heavy mist, through which the long ridge of the moor showed darkly.

The Magistrates' room was crowded, as the Coroner's room had been. There were three Magistrates on the bench, all of whom honoured the name of Belfield and sympathized with the unhappy mother, who sat apart in her black raiment, with the old family lawyer by her side. Lord St. Austell and Colonel Deverill were present, and the legal element was represented by Mr. Cheyney, the sandy-whiskered gentleman from the Treasury; Mr. Distin, who watched the case on behalf of Colonel Deverill; and Mr. Tompion, Q.C., whom Mr. Gresham had engaged to protect his client.

Markham, *alias* Melnotte, sat near Mr. Distin.

The inquiry before the Magistrates involved a

recapitulation of the evidence that had been given before the Coroner, except in the case of Sir Adrian, whose lips were now sealed, and who sat apart, with a constable standing near his chair.

The Doctor repeated his statement. Colonel Deverill once again declared his conviction that the body found in the Abbey river was that of his younger daughter, and again swore to the rings which she had worn. Again Mrs. Marrable reluctantly identified the Persian rug. The important question of identity was as fully established in the minds of the county magistrates as it had been in the minds of the Coroner and his jury.

The next question was how the deceased had come by her death.

That she had not drowned herself was established already by the evidence of the surgeon. That she had been killed by a blow upon the temple, and had been thrown in the river after death, was indisputable. Mr. Tompion cross-examined the medical witness in the endeavour to shake his testimony upon this point, but the attempt was half-hearted and futile.

Mrs. Marrable was severely handled in cross-examination by Mr. Distin. She admitted that Mr. Belfield had been disturbed in mind since his wife's disappearance, and had seemed altogether an altered man; that he had avoided the rooms his wife had occupied, and had never been heard to mention her name. All this had been thought only natural in a gentleman whose wife had run away from him. She admitted that Sir Adrian's behaviour on the morning of Mrs. Belfield's disappearance had caused some talk in the household. One of the men-servants had met him on the stairs going up to his room early in the morning, and had been struck by his dejected countenance.

"Was that before Mrs. Belfield's disappearance was known to the household?" asked Distin.

"Two hours before."

Mr. Gresham objected that this was not evidence. It was only an impression derived from another person.

"We can call the servant who made the remark," said Distin.

At this moment there was a stir and the sound

of voices at the further end of the room, near the door opening to the street, and then the crowd made way for a tall man in a furred overcoat, who came slowly up to the Magistrates' table. A silence of wonder came upon the whole assembly, which was broken only by a faint cry from Lady Belfield, who had risen hurriedly at the approach of her younger son.

" Valentine ! " she cried.

" Perhaps it would be as well to hear my account of the main fact before you waste time upon details," said Valentine Belfield.

He was pale but self-possessed, confronting all those eager faces calmly, as one whose mind had fully realized the worst that could befall him, and who was prepared to endure it.

" I am here to answer for the death of my wife," he said quietly, after the usual formula, standing like a rock, with his face towards the bench, and with an air of seeing no one but the Magistrates who sat there. " It was I who killed her."

The clerk began to take down his evidence, which

was given with a deliberation that made the writer's task easier than usual.

" Yes, it was I who killed her. She had been a loving wife, and I had been a neglectful husband, over-secure in my confidence, forgetting that there are always scoundrels and profligates on the watch for such prey—a pretty woman with a careless husband, intent on his own pleasures. We had never quarrelled, and I had never seen occasion for jealousy, till one night in a railway carriage I overheard a conversation between two men which informed me that my wife was being pursued by a notorious seducer. At first I was inclined to be incredulous, but on discovering certain facts connected with the sale of a horse which I had bought for my wife in good faith, but which had practically been the gift of her admirer, I saw that this person's intentions were as bad as they could be. The fact that he had been my particular friend would, I suppose, hardly make his conduct baser. The seducer is generally the husband's friend.

" I came down to Chadford without an hour's delay, meaning to save my wife, if there were yet time, but in no soft temper towards her. The first thing I heard upon arriving was that the seducer was living in the neighbourhood, in hiding. I entered my mother's house after midnight, with no worse intention than to call my wife to account for her falsehood and her folly, and to have a complete understanding with her. Such an explanation might have resulted in total severance, or in reconciliation. I had not asked myself which way it was likely to end. I was very angry; my heart and my head were both on fire. God knows I had no thought of killing her; but I desired nothing more keenly than an encounter with her lover.

"I found her after midnight, with her trunks packed ready for departure, all her preparations made. She was writing when I entered the room. She tried to keep the letter from me in her terror, but I snatched it out of her hand. This is the letter—unfinished."

The letter was handed to one of the Magistrates, who read it, first to himself and then aloud, amidst a breathless silence.

At the far end of the room, among the spectators, was a tall woman in black, who had entered immediately after Valentine, and who stood there watching and listening. She wore a small black straw bonnet, very plainly made, and a thick veil. Behind that veil, and in that bonnet, no one noticed Madge Darley's striking beauty. She was only one figure more in the closely packed crowd, all intent upon the man who stood in front of the Magistrates' table making a confession of his crime.

"We had some conversation after I had read that letter, a brief dialogue, which only served as a commentary on that text. She loved another man, and she had ceased to love me. She stood before me, looking me in the face and telling me that she meant to dishonour me.

"I couldn't stand this, and I lifted my cane and struck her. I suppose I meant to knock her down. I don't believe I meant to kill her."

There was a pause, and a little choking sound in his throat, before he went on very quietly.

"Unhappily, my cane had a loaded handle. I struck her on the temple, and she fell at my feet— dead. I hardly know whether she breathed after she fell, for I was unconscious for some minutes. I believe I fainted.

"When I recovered my senses my brother was in the room. He told me that my wife was dead, and urged me to make the fact public at once, and to exonerate myself from any darker crime than that of which I was guilty—the crime of an unpremeditated blow, which had proved fatal. Had I been wise or reasonable, I should have taken my brother's advice; but I was maddened at the thought of my wife's treason and my own peril. I wanted to save myself from the hazard of an inquiry. My statement might not be believed; my crime might be called murder. I thought myself clever enough to escape any question about that night's work. My wife's letter announced her intention of running away with her lover. My wife's trunks were packed ready for the journey. The world should be made to believe that she had carried out her intention.

"Unwillingly, under strongest protest, my brother looked on while I carried my dead wife through the shrubbery to the river, and threw her in at a spot where I knew the water was deepest. I took measures to weight the corpse, and it would have lain there quietly till the crack of doom had no search been made. When the business was over, I left the park, and walked all through the rest of the night. I got into Bideford next day, and took a boat, and was knocking about the coast for a week or so before I went back to the Abbey.

"No one but my brother knew of my being at the Abbey that night: no one but my brother knew of my crime. His was not a guilty knowledge. He knew nothing until the deed was done; he gave me no help in getting rid of the body; he did his utmost to induce me to confess what I had done.

"This is all I have to say."

The constable who had charge of Sir Adrian was presently ordered to take Mr. Belfield into custody; but the prisoner was treated with considerable courtesy, and accommodated with a seat while the inquiry went on. As Valentine seated himself near his brother, Adrian stretched out his hand, and the brothers clasped hands silently, amidst the silence of the court. Lady Belfield sat with her head bent and her face hidden. There was a strange conflict of feeling in her breast. Gladness because her beloved had acted an honest part, apprehension at the thought of his danger, that peril of liberty and life which he had of his own accord returned to face.

The next witness was one who had not been called previously, a witness whom Melnotte had hunted down since the inquest.

This was the man whose boat Valentine had hired on the 20th of August, and who swore to his passenger's strange manner, and the state of physical exhaustion in which he had remained for a long time.

This was the only new witness. The others repeated the evidence given at the inquest, with such additional details as Sir Adrian's counsel or Mr. Distin could extort in cross-examination.

But there was no startling effect produced by any of these witnesses. It was felt by most people present that the drama was played out.

No one doubted the truth of Valentine Belfield's confession. He was there, a voluntary witness against himself, and there was the accent of truth in every word he had spoken.

His wife's own hand acknowledged her guilty intention, and in the unfinished letter there was some justification for the husband's violence. He had done well to be angry—but he had sinned in his anger. That was all. Between the justifiable anger that would have cast off an erring wife, and the savage fury which slew her, there was a wide gulf; and that gulf had been too easily crossed by the man who had never learnt to curb his temper or to control his evil passions. That was what most people in the Magistrates' Court thought about Mr. Belfield, as the brothers sat quietly, side by side, like and yet unlike, but never truer in their allegiance to each other, come weal, come woe, than they were to-day.

The result of the inquiry was that Valentine Belfield was committed for trial at the next assizes, charged with the wilful murder of his wife, Helen Belfield, on the morning of August

20th, while Sir Adrian Belfield was set at liberty, the Bench of Magistrates choosing to ignore those points in his brother's confession which showed that though he was guiltless of being an accessory *before* the fact he was admittedly an accessory *after* the fact. Local influence and spotless character bore down the weight of evidence, and there was a murmur of approbation in the room when Sir Adrian Belfield was ordered to be released from custody. Even the fact that he had deliberately perjured himself was forgotten.

Valentine slept that night in Exeter Gaol. Lady Belfield and Sir Adrian travelled by the same train that carried the prisoner, and took up their abode in comfortable lodgings near the Cathedral, where the heart-broken mother might dwell in retirement, exempt from the publicity of an hotel, where her entrances and exits would have been watched by a score of curious eyes.

During the five weeks which elapsed before the opening of the assizes, Lady Belfield never left Exeter. She saw her son every day, and spent many hours with him in his imprisonment, comforted by the mere fact of being in his company, comforted still more by the softened temper which he showed in all things. His whole nature seemed to have been chastened by that agony of remorse which his resolute soul had struggled against in vain.

"I fancied I could forget that night, mother," he said, "blot the whole thing out, live out my life just as if no such horror had ever happened; but I did not know what the shedding of blood means. Never for one single hour of my life have I forgotten—never shall I forget, while I have a brain to remember. But I can bear the memory better now. It is not so heavy a burden."

"You have done all you could in atonement," said the mother fondly. "It was noble of you to come back."

"Noble! I should have been a contemptible cur had I hesitated, when I saw my brother's honour at stake. But perhaps I might have been that cur had it not been for a woman!"

"What woman, Valentine?"

" One who has eaten the bread of dependance in your house, mother, but as good and true and noble a woman as you who gave that bread."

And then he told his mother the story of Madge Darley's life, from his wicked wooing in the idle autumn afternoons and her steady repulse of his overtures, to his last experiences in the Forlorn Hope. He spared himself in no wise, confessing how dishonourable his intentions had been in the beginning; how true and steadfast she had shown herself from first to last.

" And yet she loves me, mother, as men are not often loved. She has loved me from the first. She loves me none the less because of this cloud upon my life. She has been to this prison once a week since I was brought here. She has come all the way from London, leaving the work which she holds sacred, and she has sat with me here, hand clasped in hand for an hour or so, and then has kissed me good-bye, and has gone quietly back to her work, travelling so many miles just for that one hour. If ever I am a free man again, Madge Darley will be my wife. Will it wound your pride, mother, that I should marry a daughter of the people?"

"My dearest, if she is as good a woman as you think her, I will welcome her as my daughter. I would be grateful to her, even if she were an erring woman, for the sake of her devotion to my son."

"She is spotless, mother, and as true as steel."

Mr. Gresham, and the famous George Tompion, Q.C., who was to conduct Valentine's defence, aided by a pair of clever juniors, had fully discussed the chances of the prisoner, and were of opinion that he would be acquitted on the capital charge. It would be a narrow escape perhaps, as the concealment of the body was a damning fact. But it was hoped that the wife's letter would influence the jury, and incline them to a lenient view of the circumstances, nor could the feeling inspired by the respectability of the Belfield family be ignored. There was no doubt that Lady Belfield's personal character would have weight with a judge and jury.

Mr. Tompion was not mistaken in this view of the case. He surpassed himself in the eloquence of his defence; he melted at his own pathos, and drew floods of tears from his audience. He dwelt on the agony of the husband's feelings, stung to madness by the treason of the wife he adored; he painted the peaceful family life—the mother with her twin sons, the domestic circle into which sin had never entered until the seducer came there like the serpent into Eden. He depicted the remorse of the unhappy man, who in one moment of madness had struck down the creature he idolized. How, in his horror at finding himself an involuntary assassin, he had tried to hide his deed from the light, had tried to forget what he had done. In vain, in vain.

"You have heard, gentlemen, that the prisoner was a changed man from that hour. He was no hardened reprobate. The pangs of conscience tortured him by night and day, and he knew not one moment of relief until he stood up before his fellow-men, and voluntarily confessed his crime, inviting whatever punishment the law might inflict."

And then Mr. Tompion went on to show that in

no case could the crime be more than man-slaughter. The act had been unpremeditated; the blow had been struck by an instrument which happened to be carried in the prisoner's hand, and to which no evil intent could attach itself. It had been the act of a single moment. The medical evidence showed that there had been but one blow, and that had been unhappily fatal. Yet it had not been necessarily fatal. Had the blow fallen upon any other part of the victim's head, it might have stunned, but it need not have killed her. There was nothing to show that the prisoner had ever contemplated her death. Had he taken his brother's advice, and at once alarmed the house, the suspicion of murder could not possibly have attached to him.

This, and much more, urged Mr. Tompion in mitigation of Valentine Belfield's guilt; and the Judge followed with a summing-up which strongly favoured the prisoner, albeit he took care to point out the reprehensible nature of all his acts after the fatal blow, and the wrong done to his dead wife's reputation and to the feelings of her kindred, in allowing her to be talked of as a runaway wife, while she was lying in her unconsecrated grave, unhonoured and unmourned. The whole course of the prisoner's conduct after his fatal act must be considered as an aggravation of the guilt of that act, said the Judge.

The result was a verdict of manslaughter. The Judge pronounced sentence—two years' imprisonment with hard labour.

It was a heavier sentence than the sanguine had hoped for; but to Lady Belfield, whose fears had been terrible, this worst and last result of her son's wrongdoing seemed light. She clasped her hands in silent thankfulness when the sentence was pronounced.

There was another woman who stood with clasped hands, full of resignation—that woman who had promised to be his wife when his hair was white. Madge Darley saw him move slowly away from the dock between two warders, and knew that for two weary years the law would hold him in subjection like a little child, meting out his tasks and regulating every movement of his life.

She knew that his slow hours would pass in automatic labours—cleaning his cell, going out and coming in at the word of command, working with a gang of other toilers, each the image of himself; eating, drinking, kneeling to pray by line and rule; living for the most part in a death-like silence, in which the ticking of the clock or the sudden opening of a door is almost too much for the prisoner's weakened nerves.

And this was all to be suffered by the spoiled child of nature and of fortune—the athlete whose life hitherto had been all activity; the sportsman to whom horse and dog and gun were among the necessaries of life; he who had been of so proud a temper, he who had never brooked control, not even the gentle restraint of love; he was to submit himself meekly to the government of a low-bred warder, to humble himself before hirelings and slaves—worse than a slave himself.

She thought of all this, sadly enough, as she lingered in the precincts of the Assize Court, waiting to question one of the officials as to the time of the prisoner's transference to Dartmoor, and the rules as to visitors there.

After waiting some time, she found a friendly sergeant, who told her the Dartmoor regulations, which seemed hard and cruel to her, who would have travelled from London to Devonshire every week just for the comfort of sitting by the captive's side for an hour, in mournful silence for the most part.

Sir Adrian met her as she was leaving the court.

" I have been looking for you, Madge," he said. " My mother would like to see you before you go back to London.   May I take you to her?"

" I should like to see Lady Belfield very much. There is no train that will take me back to London this evening.   I have engaged a room for the night, and shall go by an early train to-morrow."

" Then you can spend the evening with us. My mother wants to thank you for your devotion to my brother."

"She has no need to thank me. I have only obeyed my destiny. I could not help loving him. I loved him only the better in his misery than I loved him when he was proud and happy."

They walked together to the house in which Lady Belfield was lodging, and Adrian led Madge Darley up to the drawing-room, where his mother was sitting in an easy chair by the fire, weeping for the son whom she must see so seldom in those two unhappy years. She had seen him led off as a criminal, to become one with other malefactors. It was not enough that he had confessed his guilt, that he suffered the slow tortures of remorse. He must pay the penalty. And he had looked so pinched and haggard in the grey winter light, and afterwards in the glare of the gas. Would he live to accomplish his penance? Would he ever come forth again into the light of day a free man?

Madge went over to the sorrowing mother and knelt down beside her. Lady Belfield put her arm round the girl's neck and kissed her.

" He told me all that you have done for him,"
she said. " I thank God that there is one other
woman in the world who loves him as well as
I do."

Mrs. Baddeley stayed with her father, and
did all in her power to support his spirits
through that terrible time between the discovery
of the body and the conviction of the criminal.
Lord St. Austell went back to London immediately after Valentine's confession. He felt that
there was no more for him to do. His murdered
love was avenged. His identity with the dead
woman's lover had not been hinted at by any of
the witnesses, nor had Valentine mentioned his
name. Yet St. Austell knew that there were very
few people in England who would not come to
know that he was the man who had wrought this
evil.

So far as it was in his nature to feel sorry
for any sin of his life, he was sorry for the sin
that had brought Helen Belfield to an untimely

grave. Yet, even while remorse was still new and keen, he was capable of arguing with himself that the husband was the greater sinner—first for neglecting his wife, and then for killing her.

CHAPTER XVI.

COLONEL DEVERILL started for Marseilles directly after the trial, escorting Leo and the poodle back to London on his way. From Marseilles he meant to cross to Ajaccio, and spend the next two or three months in Corsica. It was an out-of-the-way island, where he might get a little sport, and where he was not likely to meet many of his English acquaintances.

Leonora Baddeley was deeply shocked by the events of the last three months, and even the knowledge that the kind fellow from India was on his homeward way did not suffice to restore her spirits. Everything in her life was at sixes and sevens : her creditors impatient ; Beeching inclined to be objectionable ; and the poodle's domestic comfort hardly compatible with a husband in residence, inasmuch as the dear thing always required the most luxurious easy chair in any room he occupied, and could sleep only on the fur rug by his mistress's bed, where he made the quiet night musical with his snores. There was not room for a divided duty on that small flat in Wilkie Mansions; and Leonora feared that when her kind, good fellow was restored to her, his first exercise of marital authority might be to turn her poodle out of doors.

And then, little by little, her involvements would be revealed to him ; and the butcher and the baker, and the man who had supplied her with lamps and oil to feed them, would demand their due. How was she to face those gruesome revelations : how answer to her husband for having spent four times as much as her position justified ?

She could almost have wished that the kind fellow's regiment had been forgotten by the authorities at the War Office, and left in India for the next ten years, as had happened once in the case of a distinguished regiment.

" *They* would have liked it," she told herself, " and it would have been such a relief to me."

She parted with her father at Paddington, he having refused to waste an hour in London. He was going by the night mail to Paris, and to Marseilles by the next morning's express.

"I hate London, and England, and every place that can remind me of my poor girl," he said.

He kissed his daughter in a sad farewell, and Tory stood up on his hind legs and licked the Colonel's face, deeply sympathetic, and aware that there was trouble in the family.

"He is such a clever darling," said Leo; "I'm sure he knows disagreeable letters—bills and lawyers' horrid threats in blue envelopes—for he always brings them to me with an air of being sorry for me. When shall I see you again, father?"

"I don't know. I feel utterly beaten. My life has been a failure in most ways, Leo; but this last blow has crushed me. I don't feel as if I should ever take any interest in life again. I used to regret the passage of time, hated the idea of being an old man; but now I wish I were twenty years older, with my memory gone, and my senses dim, tottering upon the edge of the grave."

"It has all been very sad for us, but it was not half so dreadful for her," argued Leo philosophically. "Think how little she suffered. A

few moments of startled surprise——one swift, strong
blow that ended life in a sudden flash, and she was
gone. She died in the zenith of her beauty, adored
by her lover. It was ever so much better a fate
than to have gone away with St. Austell, and for
him to have grown tired of her in six months, as he
most assuredly would."

"Don't talk about it," said the Colonel sternly.
"There is no consolation any way. She perished in
her youth and beauty, with her mind intent upon
sin. She had not a moment for repentance. God
be merciful to the poor light soul, and let half the
burden of her sin rest on me, because I brought
her up so carelessly, and never took pains to guide
her steps into the right way."

"It is all too sad," sighed Leo; "she might
have done so well if she had only kept her head."

Mrs. Baddeley had her burden to bear in the
way of sympathetic speeches and condoling letters
from all her particular friends, who had read and
doubtless gloated over the account of the trial.
They had pored over the unfinished letter; they

knew all poor Helen's weakness, and her intended sin; they who had envied her for the effect she had made in Society, and who perhaps were secretly rejoiced at her evil fate. Leo had to endure condolence from all comers, and to say the same set phrases over and over again. "Yes, it was all too dreadful. I believe that wretched man was half-maddened. There was always a strain of madness about him;" and so on, and so forth, till she seemed to repeat the same sentences mechanically.

"I suppose twins often *are* little queer in their heads," replied one not over wise lady.

The season was in full progress by this time, and fashionable drawing-rooms were bright with tulips and narcissi, but Mrs. Baddeley went nowhere. She wore deepest black, which looked wonderfully well against a background of yellow tulips; and she stayed at home, waiting for the good fellow from India. She had put down her victoria; or it may rather be said that it had been put down for her, since the livery-stable keeper had refused to supply her any longer with horse and man, and held her carriage in pawn while he sued her for his account. She spent her days yawning over the works of Mudie, and playing with Tory, just as she had done in Devonshire; and she took her constitutional on the Bayswater side of Kensington Gardens early every morning, before the smart people were out. She would not drive anywhere, since there was degradation in the thought of a hired vehicle, while her own pretty carriage, with its neat appointments, was locked in a mouldy coach-house under a tyrant's embargo.

Mr. Beeching called upon her, but she said not a word about the victoria. He had been somewhat sullenly disposed since his bargain with Mrs. Ponsonby and his quarrel with St. Austell. He said that he had found out the hollowness of friendship. Leo felt that there would be no good in mentioning the victoria; so she wrapped herself in the dignity of her grief, knowing that she looked very handsome in the black gown for which Jay had not yet been paid, and which fitted her better than anything of the famous Ponsonby's.

The days were drawing nigh in which she might

hourly expect her husband's arrival, and she was beginning to think about the little dinners she would give him, and how best she might soothe him, and reconcile him to Tory's existence, and to the burden of her debts.

"We shall not entertain this season," she told Beeching, "but you must come and dine here quietly whenever you can. Frank is so fond of you."

"And of a hand at *écarté*, at which he always wins," answered Beeching bluntly. "Yes, I shall like to come; Frank and I get on capitally."

It was the day after this little talk with Mr. Beeching that Leo's maid brought her a foreign telegram. The page had been sent home to his mother, as an expensive detail that must needs be suppressed in adversity.

The telegram was from Aden.

"Sorry to inform you, Major Baddeley died yesterday evening on board the *Metis*, of cerebral apoplexy. Will be buried here unless you telegraph other instructions.

"PHILPOTT, Regimental Surgeon."

The shock was severe, and there were pangs of remorse mingled with the widow's grief. She remembered how recklessly she had pursued her self-indulgent course, caring only for the pleasure or the triumph of the hour, proud of her beauty, heedless of her husband's welfare; trying always to believe that to be soldiering under an Indian sky was the best possible thing for him. She remembered with how little gladness she had anticipated his return; how willing she would have been to leave him in India till his head was grey and his limbs were feeble. And now a sterner Captain than any of the officials at the War Office had ordered him to a further shore than the uttermost border of Afghanistan or the disputed limits of Burmah.

She had sighed over the loss of her independence—had feared to stand before the only man who had a right to interrogate her; and now he was snatched away and she was free—free to make the best of her life, free in the pride of her beauty, before time had put his withering finger on a single charm.

With that telegram still in her hand she looked at herself in the glass, and told herself that her armoury was in good order. She had lost no weapon by which such women as she have power over men.

"If *he* only cared for me," she said to herself, and then she stamped her foot passionately, and crushed the telegram in her hand.

She had no one to help her. Colonel Deverill was in Corsica ; and she had no other near relation. Should she have her poor fellow brought home, to be carried into Gloucestershire, and laid in the burial place of the Baddeleys? No, the Baddeleys had never done anything for him since his father's death. He had brothers, some rich, some poor. The poor brothers had been only remarkable for dropping in to lunch or dinner on precisely the most inconvenient occasions ; the rich brothers had held themselves aloof.

"To bring him home would be dreadfully expensive," mused Leonora, "and I am almost penniless. No, he must be buried at Aden, poor dear. There is no help for it."

She telegraphed to the regimental doctor, and to the colonel, whom she knew, giving them full authority to act. And then she sent off an advertisement for the *Times*—"Suddenly, at Aden, &c. &c., deeply regretted "—in a thoroughly business-like manner; and then she sat down and cried. She wept for him honestly, after her fashion, telling herself how good he had always been to her, how easy, how indulgent; trying to persuade herself that she had been desperately in love with him at the time of her marriage, which she had never been at any time; telling herself that she would feel his loss immensely. She tried to awaken within herself all those stock sentiments which a loving wife ought to feel—and then her thoughts wandered off to the engrossing question of ways and means. Those harpy tradesmen would be more than ever ferocious now that she was a lonely widow. They would sharpen their claws to assail her. They would listen to no more excuses, wait no longer for remittances from India. They would sweep off her pretty furniture, her bamboo and beads, her Japanese jars, fans, and feathers, and embroidered portières ; all that bright-hued plumage which had made her nest so gay and pleasant to the eye of admiring man.

"They would take you, my dearest treasure, if they could" she cried hysterically, flinging herself upon the hearthrug and snatching the alarmed Tory to her breast. "But they shall never have you—no, not if you *are* worth eighty guineas and I am a pauper—never while I have life."

The announcement of her husband's death had the effect she feared, and the lawyer's letters in a day or two were more peremptory than before. There was also a shower of other letters, from condoling friends—the very people who had been continually asking, "And *where* is Major Baddeley?" "And *who* is Mrs. Baddeley's husband?" and who now wrote as if they had known and loved him, and blandly consigned him to a better world with quotations from Scripture.

Leonora had scarcely finished these customary tributes, when the maid brought her a telegram.

"Major Baddeley was buried at seven o'clock

yesterday morning, in the English Cemetery. Military honours."

"How nice," sighed Leo; "he could not have had *them* in Gloucestershire. Buried already! My poor, good-natured lamb. How dreadfully quick."

She was still studying the telegram—those few words meaning so much—when the electric bell sounded again, and the maid announced Mr. Beeching.

"I see you have had plenty of letters already," he said, glancing at the scattered correspondence on her table. "I wouldn't write. I thought it better to come."

"You are very good," she faltered, giving him her hand meekly, with lowered eyelids, remembering that he was the one man among all her intimates who could afford to help her out of her difficulties.

"I am not a humbug, Mrs. Baddeley. I'm not going to pretend that I'm sorry for your husband's death. As a man, I liked the Major well enough. He was my very good friend, and I was his, I hope.

But he was your husband, and he came betweeen me and the woman I love. Come, Leo, there's no need to beat about the bush. You have held me at arm's length for years, because you were a wife. And though I've felt that I was being fooled— for you've blown hot and cold, don't you know, led me on and held me off—yet, dooce take it, I've respected you for keeping me at a distance."

" I always knew you were generous-minded," said Leo, with a stifled sob, beginning to feel that her debts would be paid.

" You did your duty to your absent husband, and I honour you for it," pursued Beeching, admiring the beautiful head, with its dark shining hair, the heavy eyelids and long lashes, the perfect figure set off by the close-fitting black gown ; " but you are a widow now, and you are free to reward my devotion. When will you make me happy, Leo ? How soon may I call you my wife ? "

" My dear Beeching, my poor fellow was only buried yesterday."

" Yes, I know. I am not going to ask you to

marry me to-morrow. There is the world to be thought of, I suppose; though I don't care a hang about it. Will you marry me this day six months?"

"Don't ask me anything to-day. I am so utterly wretched. I cannot get that poor fellow's image out of my mind. Come to see me again in a week. I shall be calmer then."

Mr. Beeching would fain have persisted, but Mrs. Baddeley was firm, and he went.

She rose from her sofa when he was gone, and began to pace the room strangely agitated.

"To have unlimited money, a house in Park Lane or Grosvenor Place, to give the best parties in London, to have all those people who have been barely civil at my feet. They *all* worship money! Yes, that would be something. But then there is Beeching included in the bargain! To pass my whole life with Beeching—to see him every day— not to be able to send him away—to have him for my travelling companion wherever I went. Always Beeching; no escape, no variety. *That* would be terrible. Would Grosvenor Place, and a four-in-hand, and a yacht, and a large box on every first night, and everything in the world that I care for, counterbalance that one drawback—Beeching?"

She walked up and down in silence for a quarter of an hour, thinking intensely.

"I don't think I care much for money, or I should snap at Beeching," she told herself, and then in a sudden burst of passion she clasped her hands and cried: "Oh, to spend my life with the man I love, the only man I ever loved! That would be Paradise. There may be a chance even yet. He was so fond of her, and I am like her, and he cared for me first. If it is ever so small a chance, I will not throw it away."

She sat down at her desk, and wrote a telegram to Lord St. Austell, Park Lane.

"Let me see you here for half an hour on particular business. I shall wait till you come."

It was late in the afternoon when St. Austell was announced. The day was cold and dull, and in that grey light he looked ill and worn, aged by ten years since last season. He was in mourning, and his closely buttoned frock coat had a severe middle-aged air.

"You summoned me, and I have come," he said, coldly touching Leo's offered hand. "I can't conceive why you should want to see me, and I think you ought to know how it distresses me to see you." .

"I am sorry for that. I have had startling news, and I could not rest till I told you. St. Austell, I am free. My poor husband is dead. It is no longer a sin for me to talk of the past. Why cannot we both forget all the misery of last year? You were cruel to me—more cruel to that poor girl you tempted. But you may forget all——"

"Never. I have been untrue to other women. I shall be faithful to her until my dying day."

"You think that now, perhaps. You will tell a different story next year."

"I will wait for next year, and the heroine of the new story."

"And yet you once pretended to care for me," said Leo, trembling with indignation.

"It was no pretence. I did care for you—very

much at that time. Only you cared so very well for yourself, you see! You cared so much more for yourself and for your own reputation than you cared for me. Orpheus trod the burning paths of Hell in quest of his love. You would not have put your little finger in the fire for my sake; and so, finding what you were—a woman of the world, worldly to the core—I fell out of love with you, somehow, just as easily as I had fallen in love. And then your sister came upon the scene—younger, fairer, fresher, and with a heart—which you had not."

"If it pleases you to think thus of me, so let it be," said Leo haughtily. "We can be friends, I suppose, to the end of the chapter."

She looked at him piteously, pleadingly, even while her lip affected scorn. Yes, he was the only man whose accents had ever touched her heart, whose face had ever haunted her. She could have flung herself on her knees at his feet, and kissed the wasted hand which hung listlessly at his side. She could have died as Helen had died, only to be loved by him for one hour. But she knew that all was over. Of that old fire which had blazed so fiercely for a season, not a spark remained.

"Tell me about my poor friend's death?" he asked civilly; and she told him all she knew.

And then after a few trivialities, Lord St. Austell wished her good-day.

There was no help for it. It was her destiny to be burdened with Beeching.

Two years had gone by since that day in which Lady Belfield saw her son led out of the dock as a convicted felon; and she was sitting in her accustomed place by the hearth in that innermost drawing-room which was her favourite—the room that held her own particular piano, and all her chosen books. She was sitting in the spring twilight, sad and silent, but not alone in her sadness. A girlish figure sat on the fender-stool at her feet, and a month old baby was lying in that girlish lap.

There were two Lady Belfields now in the old Abbey, a mother and a daughter-in-law who never disagreed, for the daughter was just that one woman whom the mother would have chosen out of all womankind for her son's wife.

Little by little in the sad slow days after the trial a new love had grown up in Adrian Belfield's heart, and he had learnt to admire and appreciate

Lucy Freemantle's gentle character and unpretentious charms. There was no cloud upon the dawn of this new love. It came to him like the slow soft light of a summer morning, creeping up from the dark cold east, and gradually filling the world with warmth and brightness.

They had been married a little more than a year, and this happy union was the consolation of Constance Belfield's heart.

To-day that heart was to be tried by a joy that was too closely interwoven with grief. Her son was to be released from prison. He was to return to the house in which he was born, his crime expiated, his penance fulfilled; but he was to return only to die. For a long time his health had been broken. His strength had gradually decayed from the beginning of his imprisonment; and he had spent at least a third of his prison life in the infirmary. And now his mother knew that he was given back to her marked for death.

She had been permitted to see him at stated times. The hard rules of prison discipline had been relaxed in his favour. She had knelt beside his bed in the big white airy ward, and had talked with him hopefully of the days when he was to be restored to her.

" I shall go back to you an old man, mother," he said, " fit for nothing but to sit by the fire and yawn over a newspaper. I shall never hunt fox or stag, hare or otter. I shall never call myself a crack shot again. The springs are broken."

Of the contingency of non-return he had never spoken. His disease was that slow and insidious malady in which the sufferer hopes till the last. He knew that his constitution was shattered, but he did not know that his life was a question of a year or two at most.

Madge Darley went to see him as often as the prison rules allowed, and her presence cheered him like strong wine. He seemed always at his best when she was there ; and even the eyes of love were deceived by the brightness of his looks and the hopefulness of his manner. It was only when the doctor told her the hard bitter truth—one lung gone, the other attacked—that she knew how vain a dream that was upon which her lover dwelt so fondly.

He was never tired of talking of their future life together.

"I am a poor feeble creature, Madge," he said, "but at least I shall not be a hindrance to your good work. I won't promise to clean the windows, but I can write your letters and keep your accounts. You must not live at the Forlorn Hope after our marriage; but we can have a snug little villa in the Kilburn Road, and you can give twenty-four hours in every week to the good work, as the other sisters do."

She opposed him in nothing, knowing that this dream of his could never be realized. She saw the traces of gradual decay at each new visit, saw that the shadows were deepening and the end drawing nigh. She saw this and she mourned for him as one dead; but in all her sorrow she persevered bravely with the work which she had begun under such narrow conditions. The Forlorn Hope had prospered. There were three houses now in the dingy street off Lisson Grove, and there were nearly seventy ladies who each gave four-and-twenty hours in every week to the task of reclaiming fallen creatures of their own sex. The plan had answered admirably. The sisters did not renounce the world and its affections, its domestic ties, or its social pleasures. They wore no distinctive habit, they affected no asceticism beyond a strict economy. They only gave a seventh part of their lives to the task of helping the wretched : but this much they gave ungrudgingly, and with a regularity which gave way to nothing less than serious indisposition. Any sister who showed herself light-minded and inclined to play fast and loose with her duties was politely informed that she had no vocation for the work, and was requested to retire. Frivolity was thus eliminated at the outset; and, although many of the sisters were young, all were earnest workers. Some were rich and some were poor; some brought the comforts and graces of life—flowers, and hot-house fruit, and books and music, and rare old wines— from their luxurious homes, to cheer the sick and broken-hearted; some contributed largely to the expenses of the institution ; others gave only their time and labour ; but there was an equality of zeal and love which levelled all differences.

To-day Madge had gone to Dartmoor with Sir Adrian, to assist in the release of the prisoner. They had posted there and were to post back ; five-and-thirty miles by moor and road, with a rest and a change of horses midway. They were to have left the prison at one o'clock, and it was now five. They might be expected momentarily. Just as the mother had sat listening for the sound of hoofs upon the gravel, expectant of her younger son's return from hunting, so she listened and waited now.

Hark ! the steady trot of four horses. The carriage was in the avenue. Constance Belfield went out to the hall, motioning to Lucy to stay with her baby.

"I want to see him alone first," she said falteringly.

To be alone with him was impossible. The old butler and Andrew and Mrs. Marrable were there, ready to welcome the wrongdoer, almost as if it had been his return from a honeymoon. He walked a little in advance of his companions, carrying himself erect as of old, making a great effort against weakness. He shook hands hastily with the old servants, looking at his mother all the time, and then held out his arms and clasped her to his breast.

"At home at last, mother," he said, kissing the pale forehead and the soft silvery hair, which had whitened in the days of his captivity; "no more prison bars, no more galling restrictions. I belong to you and Madge henceforward."

"To me and Madge. Yes, dear. I shall not dispute Madge's claim," answered Lady Belfield, holding out her hand to the tall pale girl in black, who had once been a servant in that house, but who now entered it as a daughter.

They all went into the drawing-room, where Lucy had sent away her baby, and sat waiting for them in the glow of a great log fire, and where the tea-table was spread just the same as in the old days of the return from hunting. They sat round the hearth in a family circle, while Lucy poured out the tea; and all tried to be glad because he had come back to them, and all were full of sadness, because they knew he had returned only to die.

There is no one in London society better known than the beautiful Mrs. Beeching. Her portrait has been painted by three of the most famous Academicians, and has been exhibited for three consecutive seasons. Her dog Tory is a celebrity, and is sought after as an attraction at charity bazaars. She is one of those ladies whom people who are struggling to get into Society always endeavour to know. Her drawing-room is the gate of a second-rate Paradise, one of the outer circles of the smart world. The great family of Parvenu Pushers have climbed a long way upward on the social mountain before they begin to drop Mrs. Beeching.

THE END

PRINTED BY BALLANTYNE, HANSON AND CO.
LONDON AND EDINBURGH